Only Losers

CRY

ONLY LOSERS
CRY

SUSAN WESTLEY

TATE PUBLISHING
AND ENTERPRISES, LLC

Published by Tate Publishing & Enterprises, LLC
127 E. Trade Center Terrace | Mustang, Oklahoma 73064 USA
1.888.361.9473 | www.tatepublishing.com

Tate Publishing is committed to excellence in the publishing industry. The company reflects the philosophy established by the founders, based on Psalm 68:11,
"The Lord gave the word and great was the company of those who published it."

Book design copyright © 2013 by Tate Publishing, LLC. All rights reserved.
Cover design by Rtor Maghuyop
Interior design by Jomar Ouano

Published in the United States of America

ISBN: 978-1-62510-771-8
1. Juvenile Fiction / General
2. Juvenile Fiction / Social Issues / Homelessness & Poverty
13.01.21

DEDICATION

This book is dedicated to
the memory of
Philip J. Westley
in honor of his compassionate and
tireless work on behalf of
the homeless.
And
with deepest gratitude
to the staff of St. Matthew's House.
Their selfless work with the homeless
step by step, one day at a time,
personify their mission:
Touching hearts. Transforming lives.

For I was hungry and you gave me food, I was thirsty and you gave me drink, a stranger and you welcomed me, ill and you cared for me, in prison and you visited me.

—Matthew 25:35–36 (NAB, St. Joseph ed.)

CHAPTER 1

The slamming of the car door jolted Emily awake. The heavy boots, the crunch they made on the gravel, alerted her to danger. She curled up on the floor of the rusted Corolla. Before pulling the musty brown blanket over her head, she grabbed the wadded-up McDonald's wrappers from yesterday's dinner and tossed them on top of her. *Make it look like trash scattered on the floor*, Dad had instructed her before he left for the night.

Make it look like trash.

She added the three coffee cups on top. The smell of stale coffee made her sick. But it was the one thing that she and Dad could get free. Buy one cup and refill them at the fast-food places they passed as they traveled.

The crunch of the boots became louder and closer. Fear wrapped itself around her like a snake about to strike. Emily held her breath when she heard the tap on the window. "Anyone in there?" The glow of the flashlight cast an eerie aura throughout the car, like the moon bouncing off the fog in the cemetery where her brother, Danny, was buried. Another tap—this one even louder, more insistent. "I think it's abandoned,

Carl," the cop said. "We'll call in the tow tomorrow morning. It's a piece of garbage anyway."

The boots turned around. The sounds abated. She heard the engine of the police car spark to life and then listened to the sound of the tires as the cops backed out. Quiet descended on her. Emily remained in her hiding place, shaking, afraid to take a peek out. She began to gag at the stench of the coffee, hamburger, and greasy fries. She wanted to throw up, but moving was not an option. What if they were still there, waiting, hoping to find her?

The car door flew open with such a jolt she thought her heart would stop.

"For cryin' out loud, Em. I thought they'd never leave."

"What took you so freakin' long?" Tears threatened to spill, but Emily never cried. It was one of Dad's rules. *Only losers cry*, he told her.

He held up a red T-shirt with *Fitch NY* in yellow and a large *92* in white on the front. "And ta-da." A black hoodie, again, with *Abercrombie New York* on the front. "And check out the jeans." Dark blue and flared at the bottom. "So, what do you think? Pretty cool, huh?"

"Where did you get them, Dad? They look new."

"Never you mind where I got them." He turned to start the car and added, "We gotta get outta here before the cops come back. Ain't ya gonna thank your old man?"

"Yeah, thanks."

"Goin' to get some work tomorrow. I hear there's a guy looking for men like me to work construction over in Jackson County. Ain't we lucky?"

Lucky, thought Emily as she looked at the back of Dad's head. He hadn't had a haircut in over six months. His greasy blond hair looked brown and hung past his shoulders. He usually wore it pulled back into a ponytail a la Willie Nelson, but tonight, he looked like a bum. His red-and-black shirt was torn at the shoulder, a result of a fight he had last night in some biker bar. His dingy jeans just plain needed to be washed. When was the last time they were at a Laundromat? Last week? When was the last time they had money to wash their clothes? Or to eat?

She moved to the front seat. Dad turned the key. The engine rattled and struggled to life. They drove through three small towns. The bright neon signs passed over them, blinking and flashing like a train traveling to an unknown destination.

The lights of the last city faded. Dad turned onto a dirt road. He rolled down the windows. The song of crickets, along with the aroma of the musty night, floated through the car.

"We'll stop here for now, Em. Try to get some sleep."

The radiance of the moon sliced through the darkness. Emily climbed into the backseat. She had to curl her legs up to keep her head from hitting the door handle. She pulled the blanket up and rested her head on a pillow that Dad had gotten from the Dumpster outside the Goodwill store. She rummaged around her backpack and found Danny's small ratty teddy bear that she kept for comfort. She closed her eyes and thought happy thoughts; Mom always told her to think happy thoughts. So tonight, she dreamed of a home, of a family, of security.

"This here's my little girl, Emily. Say hi to the nice man, Em."

Emily stepped out of the shadows. She had to roll up the hems of the jeans Dad gave her last night, but the shirt and the hoodie fit. She kept her head down and mumbled, "Hi."

"Why ain't she in school?" The man's icy glare made the hairs on Emily's arms stand at attention as a prickly sensation crawled up her spine. The muscles beneath his sweat-stained T-shirt bulged like that of a body builder on steroids. He stood beside a white pickup truck full of dents.

"She's eighteen. Outta school. You got work for her?" Emily froze when she heard her dad ask.

"This is labor work, man. Nothin' for a puny girl."

Eighteen. Emily took a step back, trying to avoid the man's gaze. What a freakin' lie. In reality, she was only fifteen, but looked mature enough to pass for eighteen, maybe even twenty-one.

She started her periods when she was thirteen, the year Dad took her on the run. She kept that fact hidden from Dad. She remembered the first time she saw the blood. She stole tampons from the local drugstore.

Stealing frightened her, but she didn't know any other way to get them. It wasn't until she discovered loose change on the ground underneath the drive-in window at the local McDonalds that she had her own money. Who would drop coins and just leave them? On the nights Dad was out looking for work, or drugs, or women, she would scour all the fast-food joints in the neighborhood for coins.

She managed to get enough to buy tampons from those machines that hung on scarred walls in the roadside restrooms she would use for bathing and washing her hair. One day she found an unlocked machine. She opened it and took all the contents— enough to last three months. She didn't think this was stealing. After all, the machine was open.

"You go find something to do. I'll be back at—" Dad looked at the man.

"Six o'clock. The job's an hour away."

Emily watched Dad pile into the back of the truck with all the other disheveled men. He waved.

All she wanted to do was run away. Like her mom did. Run and find a family…be a family. Have her own room, her own bed, smell the cinnamon rolls baking in the oven. Warmth, love, protection. She had been living in the rusty Toyota for two years now. Home sweet home.

CHAPTER 2

"Hey, Em, have I got a treat for you."

Emily closed her journal and looked up to see Dad fanning himself with twenty-dollar bills. "We're goin' out to have us a real home-cooked meal tonight."

Emily smiled. "It's about time you got here. I'm starving."

They walked up the dusty road until they reached Mom and Pop's Diner. The red-and-blue neon sign lit up the darkness like a Las Vegas casino. Not that Emily had ever seen one, but Dad always said that was where they were headed. One day. The aroma of fried chicken greeted them when they opened the door. This close, the desire to eat was almost unbearable. She and Dad slid into a booth by the window.

A slender woman dressed in a pink uniform approached them. The name *Wilma* adorned a red nametag attached to a stained white apron. "The special tonight's Southern fried chicken with mashed potatoes smothered in gravy, a pile of collard greens, and homemade corn bread. Only $7.99. Pretty good deal." The waitress handed them menus.

"Sounds like a winner to me. How about you, Em?" Dad handed the menus back to the waitress.

Emily nodded. She noticed the apple pie displayed on the counter. "Can we have pie for dessert?" She looked at Dad.

"Whatever you want. This here's a day for celebratin'."

"What do y'all want to drink? Regular or sweet tea?" The waitress held up her pad and pencil, ready to write.

"I like mine sweet, if ya know what I mean." Dad winked at the waitress.

Emily rolled her eyes. "I'll have a Coke."

As the waitress left, Emily looked at her dad with his greasy hair touching his shoulders and a five-day growth on his face. "Dad, can you be a little more obvious! 'I like mine sweet.' How freakin' lame is that."

"Give me a break, Em. It's just flirtin'." Dad looked at the waitress as she walked to the next table.

"So, how much money did you make today?"

"Enough. Work was hard and dirty. We poured concrete foundations all day. I washed up a bit at Stan's gas station before comin' home."

Home? Emily thought. *A rusty Toyota's not exactly home.*

"I went to the library today," she said. "That car gets too darn hot during the day."

"Gotta be careful. Don't want no do-gooder to turn us in. Those foster homes are bad. I know." Dad stroked his chin. "Man, I need to shave. So what did ya do there?"

"I read, wrote a little, and did some drawing." Emily held up her journal.

"Let me see what you got." Dad took the journal and opened it. He flipped through the pages and shook his head. "You still tryin' to design clothes. What a waste of time."

"Got more ambition than you. I plan on going to college, designing dresses for famous actresses, and hear them say as they walk the red carpet, 'My dress was designed by Emily Anderson.' Everyone will *oooh* and *aaah*. I'll live in a mansion, have maids and a swimming pool. And my car will be in the garage, not in the woods."

"Nonsense. Where do you get such crap in your head? You'll be lucky to get a job here waitin' tables."

Emily closed her journal and placed it next to her. "You just wait and see. Living in a car sucks."

The waitress returned with their dinner. The chicken was still sizzling from the fryer, and gravy oozed down the mashed potatoes. "Can I get you anything else?" she asked.

"Just our drinks," Dad said. "Oh, and don't forget to save a big piece of pie for me and my girl here."

Emily picked up her knife and fork and sliced off a piece from the breast. Juices flowed out as she put a chunk in her mouth. She held it on her tongue for a second to savor her first meal in months that didn't come in a bag.

"Delicious." She looked up to see Dad's head bowed down as he shoveled potatoes into his mouth.

He picked up a chicken leg with his fingers and ripped a piece off the bone.

"Dad, eat slower. You've got no manners. It's embarrassing."

"Honey, this is the way a workin' man eats. Get over it." He scooped up a forkful of collards and added them to the mass of food already in his mouth.

A tap at the window made them turn. Emily saw the steely eyes first.

Dad waved to the man who had hired him earlier that day. "Hey, Frank. Come on in."

Frank shook his head and motioned for Dad to come out.

Dad wiped chicken grease off his chin, threw his napkin on the table, and rose to leave. "Be back in a minute, Em. Have some business to conduct."

Emily continued to eat as she watched Dad and Frank walk into the parking lot. Dad reached into the pocket of his stained jeans and pulled out a wad of bills. He handed Frank the money. They walked a little farther. Emily noticed Frank giving something to Dad. They shook hands, and then Dad turned and sauntered back into the diner.

"What was that all about?" Emily ran her fingers through her corn-silk hair.

"Just a little transaction, Em. Never you mind. Finish your dinner. It's time to leave." Dad took a handful of bills out of his pocket and tossed them on the table.

"But the pie."

"No time. Hurry up and finish. I got things to do."

Emily looked down at her plate, dropped the last of her corn bread in the gravy, and then scooped it up. She wiped her mouth with the paper napkin and then scooted out of the booth.

"I don't see why we couldn't have dessert. You promised." Emily pushed the door open.

"Maybe tomorrow we can get a pie."

"I thought you said this was a celebration." Emily watched the dirt fly as she kicked a stone on the dusty road.

"Shut your trap, Em. I got somethin' important to do." Dad glared at Emily as he picked up his pace.

"Everything's more important than me." Emily ran to keep up with her dad.

When they reached the car, Dad said, "Home, sweet home. Hop in the backseat, Em, and try to get some sleep. I'll be down the road a piece."

Emily pulled the blanket over herself to ward away the chill that seeped through the cracks in the doors. She closed her eyes. Before she could fall asleep, she heard someone approaching. Quickly, she dropped to the floor. As she was about to pull the blanket over her head, she heard the click of the lock and someone trying to open the door. She looked up and saw Frank, his eyes fixed on her. "What do you want?" Emily pulled the blanket around herself.

"Open the door, girl. I have something for you." His crooked grin showed an empty space where teeth should have been.

"My dad will be here in a minute."

Frank laughed. "Your dad won't be back 'til morning. What I gave him would knock a horse on its hind end."

Emily started to shiver, more from fear than from the cold.

Frank jerked the car door open and grabbed her by the arm. Emily tried to pull away and run, but he shoved her back into the car. "I wouldn't scream if I was you, little girl." He unbuttoned his shirt and began to take it off. The stench of his sour sweat made Emily retreat farther in the backseat.

She held her breath as she watched him approach. She could feel unwanted tears brimming in the corners of her eyes. Dad's words echoed in her head. *Only losers cry.* Emily knew she wasn't a loser, and she knew she needed to think fast. "Get away from me, you freak."

"Don't we have a mouth on us, little girl." He removed his shirt and let it drop to the ground.

Her eyes were drawn to the tattoo on his arm—an electric-blue dragon. Its evil green eyes mesmerized her as its fire-red tongue reached out, sensing her fear. In spite of the danger, all Emily could say was, "Did it hurt?"

"No, little girl, I won't hurt you."

"The tattoo, did it hurt?"

Keep him talking. Distract him.

Frank laughed as he loosened his belt.

The reality of the situation struck Emily. She watched Frank approach her. His hand grabbed her leg and he pulled her toward him. He unzipped his pants.

As he leaned into the backseat, her foot came up strong and swift, meeting his groin. He bolted upright, hitting his head on the door frame. Emily heard a loud crack then watched him double over and fall to the ground.

Emily grabbed her backpack and jumped out of the car. She tripped over his crumpled body as she scrambled to get away. He didn't move. Emily stood back and gave him a push with her foot. Blood gushed from the gash in the back of his head. Panic sliced through her like a warrior's rapier as she stepped back, watching blood seep into the dirt.

Ohmigod, I've killed him.

Chapter 3

Emily stood there shaking, staring at the gruesome sight. And then she ran, turning in the direction that her father had taken earlier in the evening. She ran, and ran, and ran until her lungs were ready to explode, and then she ran some more.

The sound of Dad's voice echoed in the night. "Hey, Em, where you goin'?"

She turned to see Dad sitting by a Dumpster.

"Daddy!" The relief of seeing him abated when she looked into his bloodshot eyes and noticed the pinpoint pupils. He was sweating in spite of the cold.

Cocaine again. She had seen it before. So this was more important than apple pie, more important than her. Emily sat down next to him. She wrapped her arms around her knees and cried.

His voice rough, he mumbled, "Only losers cry, Em." Then he was asleep.

The sound of growling woke Emily. The sun was sitting high in the sky. She gazed at Dad still asleep and snoring. Outside, two dogs were fighting over breakfast—a half-eaten hamburger between them. Emily's stomach began to rumble, imitating the sound made by the dogs—junkyard dogs struggling to get food, just like her and Dad. She reached into Dad's pocket, hoping he had not spent all his money on drugs. She pulled out a ten-dollar bill.

He grabbed her wrist with such force she shrieked. "What the blazes are you doin'?" His speech was slurred, and he sounded as though his mouth was full of mush.

"Dad, you're hurting me." She felt him release his grip.

"Sorry, Em. Don't sneak up on me like that." She watched him sit upright, rub his eyes, and stretch. "Where the devil are we?" He squinted, wiped dirt from his hands on soiled jeans, and looked at Emily. "Help me up. Frank's got another job for me. Gotta get to work."

"We need to get away from here. Frank's a sleaze."

"Frank's a good man, Em. He gave me work."

"He sold you coke." Emily sighed and looked up. The growling had stopped. She smiled to see that the little dog was eating the hamburger. "The small one got it. Good for her."

"What?" Dad looked at her, his bloodshot eyes beginning to focus.

"The little one. The dogs were fighting over a hamburger. The little one won."

Maybe there's hope for me. Not sure about you, Dad, Emily thought.

She spied a coffee cup being blown by the morning breeze. It flew around the Dumpster. She stood up and ran to retrieve it. "You need coffee, Dad. I'll be right back."

At the rear of the Dumpster, she leaned over to pick up the cup. Then she froze. The sound. Boots, steady, plodding. "Morning, sir," she heard a man say.

"Mornin', Officer," Dad said.

"Looks like you had a rough night," the officer said. Emily pressed herself close to the back of the Dumpster, feeling the dampness of the morning soak into her shirt. The aroma of rotten garbage made her gag.

"Just on my way to work," she heard Dad say.

"Can I see some ID?"

Emily's knees shook as she remembered more of Dad's words. *Walk away, Em. If the man comes, just walk away.* She held her breath and started walking straight—down the alleyway, behind the gas station. She never looked back.

Things I cannot change...

Emily tore open another packet of sugar and added it to the bitter coffee. Her hands trembled as she lifted the cup to her lips. She wondered if others could hear the rumbling in her stomach as the greasy smells of McDonald's sausages wafted around the corner assaulting her senses.

She had escaped. But what happened to Dad?

"Finish your breakfast. There are starving children all over the world."

Emily looked up to see a young mother coaxing her daughter to take one more bite of her meal.

How about starving children here? Emily added more cream to the coffee and grimaced as she took another sip. *How can people drink this vile stuff?*

"If you're not going to eat your breakfast, Morgan, I won't take you to the park."

Emily shook her head as the stubborn red-headed tot sat back and stared defiantly at her mom. *A mom. You don't know how lucky you are, Morgan.*

The exasperated young mother picked up her child, leaving behind an unfinished egg-and-sausage sandwich.

Thank you for not throwing it away. Emily glanced left and right before moving over to the empty booth. She picked up the remnants of food. Still warm. She took a bite and savored the saltiness of her prize.

If she was to survive, she had to have a plan. Gazing out the window at the azure sky, she ticked off her needs: First, food—St. Gerard's soup kitchen. Second, shelter—Toyota. No, she remembered Frank's body lying in the dirt and shuddered at the memory. The Toyota was not an option. Third, she had to find Dad.

CHAPTER 4

That afternoon, she put her plan into action. She headed to St. Gerard's. She and Dad had been there before. The food, provided by the local church ladies, reminded her of the meals Mom cooked.

When she arrived, Emily spotted a woman wearing a peasant skirt and a purple blouse. Two sizes too large, it hid her extended abdomen and the life within. Sidling up next to her, Emily hoped the people serving would think the pregnant woman was her mother. Today's fare was a muddy-looking stew and biscuits. The servers never looked at her as they sloshed the runny meal into a plastic bowl.

She found a picnic table and sat next to her "mother." A lady with tin foil wrapped around her head and wearing a heavy woolen coat sat across from her. Tin Lady's dark, brooding eyes never left Emily's face.

"They're watching you," Tin Lady said.

"Who?" Emily put a spoonful of stew in her mouth.

"Them." Tin Lady pointed to the sky.

Emily looked up. "I don't see anyone." She turned to the woman in the peasant skirt.

"Never mind her. She tetched in the head. Thinks that the tin foil keeps away government radio beams."

"He's looking for you," Tin Lady continued.

Emily stared back into Tin Lady's wild chestnut eyes. "Who? Who's looking for me?"

Crooked yellow teeth appeared as Tin Lady smiled and cackled.

Emily scooted down the rough wooden bench away from the creepy woman. She wolfed down the rest of her meal before throwing the bowl into a dented barrel that sat near the parking lot. She looked back to see Tin Lady staring at her. A chill danced up her spine.

Like a spectator drawn to the scene of an accident, Emily found herself heading back to the Corolla. She was aware of the dark clouds gathering. She wondered if Frank's body would be covered with bugs like the ones she had seen on *CSI*.

Emily hid in the doorway of a nearby warehouse and watched the Corolla being hoisted onto a wrecker. The driver of the tow truck threw his cigarette to the ground before entering the cab. "Who drives these things? It's not even fit for the junkyard." He slammed the door.

Standing with his hands on his hips, chewing on a blade of grass, a state trooper replied, "What'd I tell you. A piece of crap. Get it out of here before it stinks up the neighborhood."

The tow truck driver spat out the window and waved to the trooper. Emily held her breath as the wrecker began to move. She watched the trooper linger a bit longer. Her eyes narrowed as she tried to see if he was looking at Frank's corpse. But then the trooper turned away. She pressed her body closer to the entryway, afraid she would be spotted. Then she heard the crunch of his boots coming closer. A car door was opened and slammed shut. The engine roared to life, and the trooper drove off.

Her heart felt like a jackhammer as she stepped out of the doorway and headed toward the magnolia tree that had shaded the Corolla. She saw tire tracks at first; and then there it was—the blood, now dried, looking more like rusty clods of dirt. She tried to move, but all she could do was stare.

A streak of lightning pierced the dull, gray sky, followed by a deafening clap of thunder. Emily jumped. She sprinted back toward the McDonald's to avoid the drizzle but stopped when she saw the open door of an ancient church inviting her. The sign outside read, "St. Jude's Catholic Church. All are welcome."

Emily stepped inside. It felt warm, dry, and safe. She sat in the back pew.

The rain subsided, and light filtered through one stained-glass window and cast a colorful glow throughout the church. The spicy aroma of incense seemed to live in polished oaken panels that surrounded the altar. She stared at the wooden cross holding a man—his arms outstretched, his feet nailed at the bottom, head bowed in sorrow.

Is that God? I wonder if he can see me. Can he feel my fear?

She heard mumbling near the altar and observed two women with beads whispering a prayer she did not recognize.

In an alcove, a young man knelt, his head bowed before a statue of a woman with flowing robes. Flickering candles housed in red votives were lined up like miniature soldiers in front of the statue. Emily watched as the man lit one candle, crossed himself, and then left.

She opened her backpack and pulled out dry clothes. Then she slipped into the small bathroom in the back of the church and changed.

What am I going to do with these?

She placed her wet clothes in the sink.

"Time to lock up, Joe."

She cracked open the door to see a gray-haired man dressed in black speaking to another man with a belt full of keys.

"Okay, Father. See you tomorrow."

She watched Joe lock the front door and slip out a side door.

A gentle quiet descended upon the church; she heard only the sounds of cars rushing by on the street. One light glowed by the front door. Emily slipped out of the bathroom. She walked to the door and tried the handle. It wouldn't open. She turned and nearly tripped over a large cardboard box with a label that read "St. Gerard's." It was full of clothes and blankets and canned food.

Jackpot! Emily rummaged through the box until she found a blanket, a pair of jeans, and a sweater. She returned to the bathroom and gathered up her wet clothes. She lined them up on one pew to dry.

The worn cushions on the pews were comfortable and provided more legroom than the car. She looked up at the man hanging on the cross. It was a creepy sight. She decided that she should say a prayer since this was a church. Reaching into the past, she recited the only one Mom had taught her. "Now I lay me down to sleep. I pray the Lord my soul to keep. If I should die"—a shudder ran through Emily; she hated that line—"before I wake, I pray the Lord my soul to take."

Dreams flooded Emily's sleep that night. Dreams of her brother, the day he was hit by the car. Her mother, reading to her, holding her, tucking her in at night. Her dad, drunk, drugged, staggering. Suddenly, a blue dragon leaped out of the darkness and started to chase her. Blood dripped from its head, leaving a spotted trail as it came closer and closer. She started to scream as Frank's face appeared.

Emily bolted upright. Shaking and sweating, she looked around to see only the Hanging Man and the woman in flowing robes. Her only company. Her only friends.

CHAPTER 5

The church provided the ideal shelter for Emily. Parishioners were gone by six or seven. The last priest, usually the gray-haired one, left about eight; the janitor, around nine. She washed up in the bathroom, slept on the padded pews, and slipped out a side door before anyone arrived in the morning. Her plan was working.

The dollar store across the street supplied a plethora of items from food to soap to toothpaste. Cheap, but still, Emily was running out of money. She reached into her pocket and pulled out the $2.50 left from Dad's earnings. Her stomach ached, and the candy bar looked yummy. Emily picked it up and slid it into the pocket of her hoodie.

"I don't think that's a very good idea."

Emily froze. She turned, expecting to see the store manager with her hands on her hips and the SWAT team surrounding the building. But to her surprise, there stood Harry Potter, all grown up. His dark hair was slightly mussed, wispy bangs gracing his forehead. Round black glasses were perched on his nose. His deep brown eyes seemed to be piercing her soul.

"I guess not." Emily took the candy from her pocket and replaced it on the shelf. She gazed at the black shirt and the white collar that distinguished him from the famous wizard.

He smiled and said, "My name's Father Ron Meyer. What's yours?"

"Jessica," she lied.

"Well, Jessica, God doesn't look kindly on shoplifting."

"You're right, Father," she said. *Father.* Emily wondered if that was how you said it. That was how Joe the janitor had addressed the gray-haired man in black. She wasn't Catholic; she wasn't anything, but she knew a little bit about God from stories Mom read to her. Stories she heard before her brother died. Before Mom ran away, steeped in grief, leaving her with a druggie for a father. *Father.*

"Haven't I seen you before? At Mass, perhaps?" Father Ron asked.

Emily ran her fingers through her hair as she recognized him as the younger priest from St. Jude's. "I don't think so, Father. I'm not Catholic."

But I sleep there at night after everyone's gone.

"Well, Jessica, you know you're welcome anytime, Catholic or not."

Emily watched the priest turn and leave. She reached for the candy bar and once again slipped it into her pocket.

She left the store and followed the priest across the street. Climbing the stone steps, she hesitated before opening the large wooden doors to the Gothic-style church. The sunlight bounced off stained-glass windows, providing an array of rainbows—a sign of peace.

She sat in the last pew and unwrapped her candy, stuffing the paper in her pocket instead of dropping it on the floor like people did in movie theaters. The chocolate melted in her mouth, the sweetness lingering. She didn't want to leave the protection of the church but knew she would be back that night—before the custodian locked the door—hiding, waiting, wondering if she would ever get caught.

Unsatisfied with just the candy bar, Emily made her way back to the soup kitchen.

The strong odor of garlic filled the cafeteria at St. Gerard's. Lasagna from good Samaritans at the local Methodist church, along with large hunks of garlic bread, sat beckoning the hungry. Before entering the cafeteria line, she scanned the tables. No Tin Lady. She picked up a tray, a Styrofoam plate, and the plastic utensils provided. Cheese oozed out of the piece of lasagna that a woman dressed in frilly pink placed on her plate. Sauce seeped into the crusty bread as Emily made her way to one of the long tables.

As she ate, she thought about a Help Wanted sign she had seen at a local Denny's just a couple of blocks from St Jude's. Denny's would be a good place to start job hunting.

CHAPTER 6

"I want to see your social security card." The manager stood behind the counter, looking at her application.

"I know the number. Just can't find my card." Emily was getting good at deceit.

"Can't hire you without some kind of identification." The manager handed back her application.

"What am I going to do? I need a job."

"Try the store next door. They usually need help." The manager turned to smile at a couple entering the restaurant and then added, "Ask for Miki."

Emily walked to the store next door. The words "Miki's Asian Treasures" decorated the front window. She looked at her reflection and tucked in her shirt before entering. She noticed a spot on her jeans and licked her fingers and tried to rub it off. She definitely needed money for the laundry.

An Open sign greeted her, along with the chime of a tiny bell, as she pushed open the door. A tiny woman with shiny black hair twisted into a bun stood arranging jewelry on a shelf near the back of the store. "Can I help you find something?"

"I'm looking for Miki," Emily said.

"You found her. I'm Miki Jarrell. What can I do for you?" The woman smiled; her almond eyes twinkled as she took a step toward Emily. She wore a flowing red silk kimono whose hem graced the tops of her tiny feet. Delicate golden flowers were stitched throughout the robe, which was belted at the waist with a black obi.

"The manager next door said that maybe I could work for you. I'm looking for a job."

"Do you have a name?"

"Jessica. Jessica Jones." The lies were getting easier and easier.

"Well, Jessica Jones, you look a little young to me."

"I'm seventeen and have my GED."

"Do you have any experience?"

"Just babysitting. I used to babysit my brother when my mom and dad worked. I work real hard. Honest."

"Well, I could use someone to clean the shelves a couple days a week and unpack the Friday deliveries. I'll pay you $9 an hour."

Emily smiled and nodded. "That sounds great. When can I start?"

"Right now. I'm sick of this cleaning and need to get some work done in the back room." Miki handed Emily a dust rag. "Let's see what you can do. Why don't you start over there? If you like the job, I will get the paperwork ready for you to sign."

Miki disappeared. Emily walked over to the first shelf and started to dust a fat Buddha that sat laughing at her.

Cool, I did it. But the paperwork part scared her. She needed to think fast.

As the day rolled by, Miki appeared only at the jingle of the bell. No paperwork materialized.

When Emily finished the last of the dusting, she heard a sizzling sound and smelled the scrumptious aroma of pork coming out from a curtained door that hid the back room. Curious and hungry, she peered through a small gap to see Miki standing over a wok. On a large cutting board sat thin slices of onion and green and red pepper, along with a bowl of juicy pineapple.

Miki turned around. "Hungry?"

Emily stepped in and watched her fling the vegetables in the wok, stirring them along with the pork. "Yes. I haven't eaten since lunch."

"Do you like sweet and sour pork?"

"Never had it. I go for burgers and fries most of the time."

"Well, it's about time you tried something different. Dishes are in the cabinet over there." Miki pointed to a red lacquered cabinet rich with scenes of mountains and trees and a man on a horse. "You'll find everything else in the top drawer."

Emily traced the edges of the flowers that were etched on the side. "It's so beautiful."

"It belonged to my great-grandmother. She used it to store her linen. Tell me about yourself and your family."

Butterflies flitted in Emily's stomach. "We don't have anything as nice as this." She pulled the brass handles on the doors to see china plates decorated with a dainty pastel-pink floral pattern.

"Don't forget the teapot and two cups."

"Do you eat here every night?" Emily picked up a vintage china teapot that had a matching floral design scatter across it.

"No, my husband's working tonight. And you looked like you could use a good meal."

At the table, Emily looked down to see chopsticks—no fork.

What the heck? What do I do with these things? She watched Miki take a bite. Emily picked up the chopsticks, but no matter how she held them, her food kept falling back onto her plate.

"I guess a burger-and-fries girl has never used chopsticks before." Miki stood and walked to the red cabinet to retrieve a knife and a fork.

"I could learn," Emily said, but Miki laughed and handed her the utensils.

Emily chewed each bite, relishing the delightful sweetness of the pork as it mingled with the crispy vegetables. "This tastes really good," she said.

"Thank you. Tell me about yourself, your family," Miki prompted again.

"Not much to tell. My dad's deployed. He flies helicopters in Afghanistan. I'm staying with my mom and grandmother until he comes home."

"When will he return?"

"Sometime next year. Everything he does is super secret."

"Do you live close by?"

"Not too far away." Emily needed to change the conversation—fast.

A small ringing sound interrupted their talk. She heaved a sigh of relief as Miki reached for her cell phone, lifted the lid, and said, "It's Da-Shawn. I need to take this."

Emily took the opportunity to put the last of her food in her mouth, close her eyes, and savored her first real home-cooked meal in months.

When Miki came back, she looked down at Emily's empty plate. "Would you like more? There's plenty."

Emily nodded and watched her spoon more brown rice on her plate and then smother it with the last of the meat.

After dinner, Miki handed Emily a fortune cookie. "Let's see what it says. Perhaps you will have some luck today."

Being here is the luckiest thing that's happened to me in a long time.

Emily broke the cookie and took out the tiny paper snuggled within. She looked at Miki before reading the prophecy. She read aloud, "'Be prepared to accept a wondrous opportunity in the days ahead.'"

"That's a good one." Miki snapped her cookie open and read, "'A pleasant surprise is in store for you.' I love surprises. Don't you?"

Emily thought of the night Frank surprised her and said, "Good surprises."

"Come on, help me clean up. It's time to go home. Oh my gosh, I forgot to have you fill out the paperwork.

I guess we can do it tomorrow. Here's the money I owe you today."

Emily took the bills and stuffed them in her pocket. "Thanks."

"Will you be able to come in tomorrow? Say, by nine o'clock?"

Emily nodded. "I'll totally be here."

CHAPTER 7

The click of the lock echoed through the empty church. Opening the bathroom door, Emily peeked out to make sure everyone was gone. A check of the St. Gerard's box revealed a new down-filled pillow. It wasn't stealing. After all, it was donations to the poor, and Emily, for sure, fit that category. She pulled the $32 she earned that day out of her pocket and counted it for the fourth time.

She snuggled up in her pew-bed and looked up at the man hanging on the cross. She rummaged around in her backpack and took out her journal and her teddy bear. The stubby pencils in the back of the pew were sharp and ready for use. She flipped through her journal, stopping at the recent sketches.

A waitress, Dad? No way. How lame is that? A designer, definitely.

Emily turned to a fresh page. Pencil in hand, she quickly sketched the Hanging Man on the blank page. But this time, he was smiling, with his long chestnut hair resting on his shoulders. She bit the end of the pencil, tilted her head, and started to write,

> I'll start with the good news: Got a job today.
> And finally some money. My boss is Miki. She
> seems nice. But the bad news: I have to fill out
> "paperwork." I guess I can lie—again. Make
> up a social security number. But what if I get
> caught? Juvie? A foster home? No way.

Before closing her journal, Emily turned to a fresh
page and sketched a picture of a kimono. Then she
tucked her journal away and put her head on the pillow.

The Hanging Man appeared to open his eyes and
stare at her. *Okay, okay,* she thought. *Now I lay me
down...* Hugging her bear, she fell into a fitful sleep
before finishing her prayer.

Again, unwanted dreams flooded her night. The
Hanging Man got off the scarred wooden cross and
started walking toward her. No, it was more like
floating. He reached out a hand to her, and she tried
to touch him; but he disappeared, to be replaced by the
dragon. She jerked awake, shaking and sweating. She
looked at the cross to see the Hanging Man still on his
wooden perch, his head bowed, quiet.

Unable to sleep, Emily decided to explore. She
tiptoed past the altar and entered a door near the right,
at the back of the church. Walking through a narrow
hallway, she encountered stairs leading downward. A
faint glow from a light gave her courage to descend.
With each step, the creaking of the wood echoed off the
empty walls. Fear crept in as she reached the bottom.

Maybe this isn't such a good idea after all.

But curiosity drove her farther. A small dark room beckoned. It burst to life when she flipped the light switch. Pictures of men and women in robes covered the lime-green walls. Saints—some holding crosses, one with a bird on his outstretched hand—surrounded her. In the corner stood a statue of the woman in the flowing robe, smaller than the one in the church. She touched the woman's hand, half hoping that she would move.

Crazy. I'm freakin' losing it.

A *clang* rang out when she tripped over a metal pail. She fell into mops and brooms leaning up against another wall. She froze, wondering if the racket would alert someone to her presence. She held her breath, listening. Nothing. She turned to leave and bumped into a desk littered with paper. The glow of a laptop greeted her.

Ohmigod, it's on.

Emily pulled out a battered leather green chair and parked herself in front of the small computer. She took a deep breath before hitting the small blue symbol that would transport her to the Internet.

Okay, Dad, let's see what happened to you.

Click. She pushed the blue symbol.

First, she searched Google to find the website for the Jackson County Sheriff's Department. Scrolling down to view her choices, Emily stopped at "Find Out Who's In Jail."

Her heart started to beat a little faster.

Click. A list of dates popped up. She scrolled down to July 18.

Click. So many faces. Young faces, old faces, men with long hair or no hair at all, women with short snarled hair. Blank eyes staring into an indifferent camera—sad, forlorn expressions; one was sneering. No smiles in these photos.

Her hand froze on the mouse when Dad's photo popped onto the screen. His bloodshot eyes, disheveled long hair, and scruffy beard stared at her. Heart racing, she read through the offenses:

Loitering or prowling

Narc equip paraphernalia (possession and/or use)

Emily's hand flew to her mouth when she read further. His release date was one year away.

She pushed herself away from the desk and stared at Dad's face—frozen in time for anyone who cared to see. Instead of feeling loss or loneliness, Emily felt relief. At least she knew where her dad was. But now she must confront a new problem. How was she going to survive for a year?

Well, doesn't this just suck? Crap, Dad. Now what?

Emily made her way back to her pew-bed. She wrapped herself in the blanket and tucked the teddy bear under her arm. She stared at the Hanging Man until her eyes closed, and she slept without nightmares or worries or fear.

CHAPTER 8

A clank and the sound of footsteps approaching jolted her from sleep. Emily dropped to the floor, gathering up courage to peer over the top of the pew. The jingling of keys and the humming came from somewhere close by. She peeked around the corner to see the janitor sweeping the floor in front of the altar.

How could I oversleep?

She stuffed her pillow and blanket beneath the pew, along with her backpack, and crawled up the side aisle to avoid detection. She found refuge in a small, dark room on the side of the church. She trembled.

What if someone finds me?

Suddenly, a small window opened. Emily held her breath. Someone was in the room next to her.

She peered through the window but could see only the profile of a man.

She reached for the door handle and turned it slowly. It rattled, and she heard the man in the next room say, "May the peace of Jesus Christ be in your heart and on your lips to make a good and holy confession."

Emily froze. *What in the world is he talking about?*

"Good morning," he whispered. "Do you need help?"

Emily stammered. "I'm not sure…I just…I just want to get out of here." The walls of the room closed in, smothering her.

"Is this your first confession?" the shadowy figure in the next room asked. "It's okay. I'll assist you. Let's make the sign of the cross together. In the name of the…"

Realizing that it was Father Ron, she felt her heart begin to pound and her chest heave as if she had just finished a mile-long run. The fear inside of her, the loneliness began to swell. Uninvited tears found their way to the corners of her eyes. *Only losers cry*, Dad's mantra echoed in her brain. But as though there was a tiny crack in a dam, the tears began to flow, and she was unable to stop the raging surge. The dam burst, giving way to a flood of sobs. "I don't…know how…to do that."

There was silence in the next room. Emily could see the priest turn and say, "Jessica, is that you?"

She nodded her head. "Yes—well, no, my name isn't Jessica. I lied, Father," she confessed. "My name is Emily."

"Take a deep breath and tell me, why are you sitting in the confessional?"

"I'm freakin' hiding."

"Well, you picked an interesting place to hide." She heard laughter in his voice as he continued. "I give you a B plus in confessing. Is there anything else on your conscience?"

Emily didn't know how to respond, but then blurted out, "That candy bar. You know, the one in the dollar store? I stole it."

"Hmm, now that's something we can sink our teeth into." Even Emily had to smile at that one. "Anything else?"

"No, that's it for now. I'm out of here." Emily placed her hand on the door handle.

"Not yet. Are you sorry for what you did?"

"Yeah, I guess."

"Okay, bow your head while I give you absolution." She heard Father Ron mumble words that were foreign to her then added, "Okay, let's say the Act of Contrition together."

Emily didn't know what to do, so she said, "Now I lay me down to sleep…"

Father Ron chuckled and said, "Let's go into the church. You can start at the beginning and tell me what's going on."

"No, Father, I'll leave."

"Perhaps I can help, Jessica…um, Emily. Give me a try. I'm a good listener and great at keeping secrets." She watched the priest rise and open the door on his side of the confessional. Then he opened hers. "Come on, don't be afraid."

They sat side by side, both silent, both staring at the Hanging Man. "I give you my word as a priest, anything you tell me I will hold sacred. No one will ever know." Father Ron turned to face Emily.

Her foot wouldn't stop wiggling and she started to twist the end of her hair. Then the words tumbled out like a waterfall after a torrential rain. She could no longer stop them anymore than she could stop the destruction of a tornado racing toward her home. "It all started the day my brother died. He was hit by a car. It was my fault. I was babysitting him and let him go out to ride his bicycle. He wasn't supposed to, Father, but he begged me."

The kind priest took Emily's hand. "You couldn't have known."

"But my parents said it was my fault. My mom cried for weeks and then one day she was gone. My dad…my dad…drank…and drank. He said it dulled the pain. He used to smell like Old Spice, but now just sweat, beer, and weed."

"Where is your dad now?"

"Jail."

"Are you sure?"

"Totally."

"Who is taking care of you?" Father Ron's gentle brown eyes made her tear up again.

Emily sniffed and wiped her nose. "Me."

She stood and walked over to her pew-bed. Reaching underneath, she pulled out the blanket and pillow. "This is my home until I get enough money for an apartment. How lame is that?"

Father Ron pushed his Harry Potter glasses up on his nose. "Lame? I'd say clever. How old are you, Emily?"

"Eighteen."

Father Ron wrinkled his forehead. "The truth."

Emily bowed her head and whispered, "Fifteen." Then she looked the priest in the eyes and continued, "But I have a job. If you let me stay here, I know I will have enough money in a few months to get a place of my own. Please, Father."

"Where are you working?"

"At Miki's Asian Treasures. It's five blocks from here."

"I know Miki. She's a parishioner. Do you mind if I talk to her? I have an idea."

CHAPTER 9

The ringing of the bell sounded louder this time. "We don't open until ten o'clock." Emily heard Miki call from the back room.

"Miki, it's Father Ron. I need to talk to you."

Miki parted the curtain and stepped into the store. Instead of the red kimono, she wore a casual pair of black silk pants topped with a yellow-and-orange-flowered jacket. Her smile turned into a frown when she saw the pair standing in the doorway.

"Jessica. Father Ron. What's going on here?"

"We need to go into the back room and talk," Father Ron said.

"Sure, but Jessica—"

"Her name isn't Jessica, Miki. It's a long story." Father Ron looked at Emily. "Are you okay with this?"

Emily nodded and watched the two disappear through the curtain. While she waited, she paced the aisles, stopping only to straighten the laughing Buddha and open and close the many colored fans on the shelf next to him.

It's taking forever. Now I've lost everything. I should have kept my mouth shut and run.

She strained to hear their conversation, but the only sounds coming from behind the curtained door were whispers.

When they walked back into the store, neither Father Ron nor Miki was smiling. Emily's heart began to pound, and she felt a rising tightness in her chest.

Father Ron spoke first. "I think we have found a temporary solution to your situation."

Emily held her breath.

Miki reached out and took her hands. "You can't live on the streets. It's too dangerous. I want you to stay with me and my husband while we figure out what to do next. How does that sound?"

Emily remained silent. Her heartbeat slowed, but her mind was racing. "Are you sure your husband wouldn't mind?"

"I called Da-Shawn and explained the situation to him. It's fine with both of us. It's the best thing, Emily. And you can continue to work in the store. But because of your age, we're forced to contact family services."

Emily took a deep breath and shook her head. "Not family services. Please. They'll put me in a foster home."

"Don't worry. I have a few more tricks up my sleeve." Father Ron winked at Emily and then turned to leave.

"You can trust Father Ron," Miki said. "You are one brave girl. Everything is going to be all right."

Emily sighed. *Trust* was a word that didn't exist in her vocabulary—not since her brother died, not since her mom left, and definitely not since Dad took her on the run. How could she trust these people? She didn't even trust herself.

The earthy scent of sandalwood mixed with spicy ginger was the first thing Emily noticed when entering Miki's home that afternoon.

"Here's your room." Miki opened the door.

Rose-colored wallpaper covered the entire space like a giant gift. A midnight-blue comforter, smothered in delicate cherry blossoms, covered a small bed in the corner. An antique white chest of drawers stood near a window dressed in fuchsia sheers. Sunlight flooded the room. A stack of boxes sat in front of the closet.

"It's beautiful." Emily stroked the bed and watched a bird land on the tree outside. Turning to Miki, all she could say was, "Thank you."

"You're welcome. It belonged to my daughter." Miki walked over to the dresser and picked up a silver frame and handed it to Emily.

Emily gazed at the raven-haired girl. Her skin was darker than Miki's ivory complexion, but the almond eyes reflected her mom's. "Is she in college?"

"No." Miki looked down. "She was killed. February fourteenth, three years ago, by a drunk driver. It was the night of the school's Valentine dance. The roads were icy. Joy forgot to fasten her seatbelt. The driver was distracted—busy texting."

Emily replaced the picture on the dresser. "Oh. I'm sorry."

Sorrow flooded Miki's eyes like dark clouds passing before the sun. "It was my fault. I gave her permission to ride there with friends. I shouldn't have done it.

Da-Shawn fought me on it. But she begged, and I gave in. Joy would be here if not for me."

Emily thought of her brother as she searched for comforting words. "You couldn't have known."

"Da-Shawn took it the hardest. He was working in ER when they brought her in. He still has nightmares." Miki hugged herself and rubbed her arms as if an Arctic breeze had blown through the room.

Emily walked over to Miki and embraced her tiny frame. Consoling another felt awkward, yet somehow comforting.

"Well, enough talk of that," Miki said, returning Emily's hug and shaking off gloomy thoughts. She pushed the boxes away from the closet and opened the door. "I've finally had the courage to pack up Joy's things. There's plenty of room in the closet for your clothes."

Emily opened her backpack and pulled out the jeans that she had plucked from the box at St. Jude's. She turned to see Miki holding a tattered pink organza dress full of brown stains. Miki kissed it and quickly stuffed it in the top box. "This was the dress Joy wore that night. I have kept it for way too long. I couldn't… didn't want to let go."

Emily looked down to see Danny's teddy bear staring up at her from the bottom of her backpack. She reached in to stroke the soft fur. *I know what you mean.*

Miki handed Emily some hangers. "You know, we're going to have to make some official arrangements if you're going to stay here. Father Ron has a friend at family services, so he's going to talk to her."

"Does he know everyone in this town?" Emily asked.

"Almost." Miki smiled.

Emily shook her head. "Can't I stay here just for a little while? If you let me work, I can get enough money for an apartment."

"You're only fifteen, Em. It's impossible. Father Ron's looking into this for us. Honest, you can trust him."

That night, Emily pulled her journal out from her backpack. Then she rummaged around the tiny desk to find a pen.

> First the good news. I have a safe place to stay. Miki's letting me crash for a while at her house. But the bad news: I'm staying in a dead girl's room. Miki's daughter was killed a few years ago and her clothes are sitting in boxes. Still in the room. How creepy is that? The dead girl has some pretty awesome clothes (I peeked in the boxes). But OMG, when her mom pulled this dress out of the closet, I almost freaked. It's ripped in a couple of places and has rust stains on it. Eww, I think it's blood. Double creepy. The worst news: I'm sure do-good social workers are going to show up and take me away. I'm supposed to trust Father Ron. I know he's a priest, but trust?

Before closing her journal, Emily looked at the framed picture of Miki's daughter and sketched her. She thought about how much fun it would be to go to a school dance, something she would never experience.

If I ever get to wear a fancy dress, it would look like this. She began drawing formal dresses. *Move over, Vera Wang. Emily Anderson is so taking over!*

That night, the silky sheets and the soft bed provided her a dreamless sleep. No floating men. No dragons. No evil men.

CHAPTER 10

The next morning, Emily woke to the smell of bacon. She watched the light stream in through the window. The tweet of the bird perched on a branch of the magnolia tree outside made her smile. For the first time in weeks—no, years—she felt safe. She reached for the blue silk robe Miki had given her and plodded barefoot downstairs to the kitchen.

She spotted a large man standing over the stove cracking eggs into a pan filled with hot butter. He wore faded-green scrubs. The tattoo of an anchor was etched on an arm the color of dark chocolate. Emily jumped when he turned and spoke. "You must be Emily. I'm Da-Shawn Jarrell. Have a seat." Then he frowned and added, "How's my Miki treating you? You look like you could add some meat to that skinny frame of yours if you want to keep up with her demands."

"Are you a doctor?" Emily pulled out a folding chair and sat down.

"No, I'm a nurse."

Emily giggled. "You look more like a football player than a nurse. I didn't know men were nurses."

Da-Shawn rolled his eyes. "I played football with my crew in the navy. And of course, men can be nurses. Don't be so sexist."

"So I see you two have met."

Both turned as Miki stepped into the kitchen. "Where's my plate?" She kissed her husband and sat at the table.

"Hold on, woman, I need to feed our guest here before you start working her to the bone."

The loving banter between Da-Shawn and Miki made Emily grin.

Da-Shawn filled three plates with warm eggs cooked sunny side up, bacon, rye toast, and something that looked like cream of wheat.

"What's that white stuff?" Emily asked.

"Grits. Ever eaten any?"

Emily stirred them with her fork. "No, can't say I have."

"Give them a try. You'll like them."

Emily took a forkful. She hesitated and then put it in her mouth. She wrinkled up her nose and said, "Feels like mush and tastes so lame."

"Here, add a bit of butter and some salt and pepper." Miki handed her the salt shaker.

"You sound like a Yankee. Where you from, girl?" Da-Shawn asked.

"I was born in Upstate New York. But I have been living around…"

Da-Shawn nodded as he poured two cups of coffee and filled three glasses with orange juice.

"Such service from a handsome man," Miki said.

"A pleasure, pretty lady." He bowed before kissing Miki on the top of the head. "Dig in, Em. Miki's a slave driver. You need all the nourishment you can get."

Miki swatted Da-Shawn on the arm and laughed.

During breakfast, Emily listened as Da-Shawn told Miki about his night in ER. "There was a terrible accident on I-75. It was a mess. A carload of teenagers speeding. Driver lost control. And, Miki, after all the news and warnings, none of them were wearing seatbelts. It was a miracle that they came away alive. Badly hurt, but alive."

Miki shook her head. "Just like the night Joy died. If only she'd worn her seatbelt. Maybe she'd be here today."

Silence blanketed the room. Finally, Emily said, "Thanks for the great breakfast, Mr. Jarrell."

"It's Da-Shawn. And you're welcome." He smiled. "Eat up, girl. If I know my wife, you have a busy day ahead of you.

Before leaving, Miki reminded Da-Shawn, "The man is coming this morning to fix the washing machine. Don't fall asleep before he arrives, or you'll be down at the river beating your scrubs with a stone."

Emily watched Da-Shawn roll his eyes and say to his wife, "Woman, have I ever let you down?"

As Emily and Miki pulled out of the driveway, they noticed a dented white pickup truck rolling down the street. When they passed it, Emily shuddered at the sight. The glare of the morning sun masked the silhouette of the driver, but there was something familiar about the dragon staring at her as his arm dangled out of the window.

Miki looked in the rearview mirror as they drove past. "Looks like Da-Shawn will get to sleep this morning after all. The workman is here early."

"Who is that guy?" Emily felt goose bumps form on her arms and legs.

"Some handyman Da-Shawn treated in ER early this summer. Does good work."

"You've used him before?" Emily turned around to see the white truck turn into the Jarrells' driveway.

"Yeah. He's good. I had him paint the bathrooms and repair a closet door. He is what you'd call a jack-of-all-trades."

"You trust him?"

"Sure. Why wouldn't I?" Miki turned the corner. "Do you know him?"

"No. He just looked like someone my dad used to know."

Chapter 11

While dusting glass figurines at the back of the store, Emily's thoughts focused on the tattooed arm that dangled from the window of the white pickup. She tried to shake the image from her mind, but the memory of that awful night kept pushing and pushing. His evil grin, the polluted stench of his sweaty body, the fear, the danger—they all still haunted her.

Impossible, she thought. *That dirtbag's dead.*

The crashing sound of a bronze Chinese dragon reverberated throughout the store. Emily jumped as it landed on her foot. The pain of the heavy object made her cry out.

Miki rushed out of the back room. "Are you okay?" The dragon stared up at them.

"I'm good. Sorry. I don't think it's broken." Emily bent down to retrieve the statue and handed it to Miki.

Miki turned it over and said, "No harm done. Did you know that this dragon symbolizes honor and power and safety?"

Emily shook her head.

"People believe it will protect their homes if they place it in a window. Why don't you put it in the window by the Buddha? We could always use a little protection."

Emily took the figurine from Miki and walked toward the front of the store.

Without warning, the hairs on her arms stood up as a prickling sensation passed over her. The dragon seemed to sizzle in her hand, warning her. She looked up to see Tin Lady walking toward the store. Gray hair poked out of the spaces in the foil, making her look like a person coming in from months of wandering through the wilderness. She was pushing a shopping cart filled with brown paper bags, a red blanket, two pillows, and a broom. Emily ducked behind the shelves as Tin Lady stopped to gawk at the newly placed object.

The front door creaked as the tiny bell jingled.

OMG, this can't freaking be happening.

Miki shouted from the back, "Can you get that, Em?"

Emily hurried into the back room. "You need to come out, Miki. It's a crazy person trying to get in."

"I'll bet it's Alice. Is there aluminum foil wrapped around her head?" Miki asked.

"And she has a shopping cart full of junk," Emily said.

Miki smiled. "Come on, I'll introduce you. She's just a poor soul wandering the streets."

Emily watched Miki embrace the ragged woman and then reach behind the counter. She pulled out a sweet roll and handed it to the bedraggled woman.

"Alice, meet Emily Anderson, my new friend. Emily, meet Alice Reynolds, my best customer."

Emily nodded as Alice stared at her.

"You must be careful." Alice took a step toward Emily, who frowned and tried to back away. "Danger is all around."

"Danger?" Emily asked.

This woman is a total whack-job. She scares the crap out of me.

Tin Lady frowned and took another step closer. Her breath reeked like the discarded garbage from the diner next door. "Be wary. He's out there."

"You're creeping me out." Emily's eyes opened wide, and she turned to Miki. "She is so spooky. What is she talking about?"

"Never mind Alice. Some say she's a psychic." Then she whispered, "But she's a little off." Miki tapped her head.

Emily nodded. *Off? More like a freakin' mental case.*

"Go in the back room, Em," Miki continued. "There's a statue of a little dog on the shelf by the refrigerator. Get it for me. I want Alice to have it. It'll remind her of the shaggy brown mutt that was her constant companion. It was hit by a car over a year ago, and Alice still mourns it."

When Emily returned, glass dog in hand, Tin Lady was pushing her cart down the paper-strewn alley. Emily looked at Miki. "Want me to go after her?"

"No, she'll be back. I like to give her a little something every time she wanders in. No one cares for the poor dear. I worry about her on the streets all alone."

Business was slow that morning. Emily finished dusting the shelves and stocking the Friday merchandise. She helped a customer pick out lanterns for a party and then called to Miki to ring up the purchase.

"You do it, Em. I'm in the middle of counting fans."

Emily pushed the keys and watched the drawer open. The shopper handed her a twenty-dollar bill. Reaching into the drawer, Emily counted out the change for the customer. Before closing it, her eyes lingered on the cash housed in their separate niches.

Miki won't miss a couple tens. Emily removed two crisp bills, but before she could stuff them in her pocket, she heard, "What are you doing?"

Her hand started to shake as she turned to face Miki. "Nothing."

Think fast.

"I was just straightening the money."

Miki frowned.

Emily continued "I…um…was going to come in the back and get some change from you. We need fives."

Miki walked to the register and counted the money. "We have enough fives. Why don't you put the money back in the drawer and close it."

Emily nodded. Her hands were still shaking as she returned the money to the drawer.

Oh my gosh, that was close.

"It's almost time for lunch. Father Ron said he'd meet us around twelve thirty. Wash up. You never know where that money has been."

Or where it was going, Emily thought.

Emily stepped into the small bathroom near the back door. She looked at her pale face in the mirror. *Have you totally lost your mind? Way to screw up, you idiot.*

She turned on the water and scrubbed her hands to try to wash away the stain of stupidity. *Taking that money was the lamest thing you've done yet,* she scolded herself.

Returning to the front of the store, Emily heard the click of the lock and watched Miki rotate the sign, indicating they would be back at two o'clock.

Miki turned around. "Ready?"

"Almost." Emily grabbed her backpack and slung it over her shoulder. Her journal tumbled out and fell to the floor.

Miki reached down to pick it up. "You keep a journal?"

"Yeah."

"I have one myself. I started it the month after Joy died. A grief counselor told me it would help."

"Did it?" Emily took the tattered diary from Miki and tucked it in the large pocket in the front of her backpack, zipping it for security.

"Yes, a little. But the sorrow never really goes away."

Emily thought about her brother, her mom, and her dad—another part of her life she couldn't explore. It still carried way too much pain. *God, will it ever go away for me?*

Chapter 12

Emily looked through the large windows surrounding the '60s-style diner and spotted Father Ron sitting in a booth with red vinyl seats, his hands folded on the shiny black table. She tapped on the window and grinned when he looked up and gave her the peace sign.

Upon entering, Miki waved to a neighbor sitting across the room as she and Emily headed to the booth. Father Ron stood, hugged Emily, and kissed Miki on the cheek.

A folder thick with paper lay on the table. "I've asked Mrs. Garcia to join us. She's a case worker with DFS." Father Ron opened the file to reveal a brochure with a picture of a mother cradling a baby and a dad holding the hand of a small child.

Emily's heart quickened. DFS, the Department of Family Services, her biggest fear. "Do we have to meet so soon? What if they put me in foster care?"

"Mrs. Garcia's a friend and parishioner." Father Ron opened a menu. "You can have faith in her, Em."

"Is there anybody you don't know?" Emily shook her head. She watched Father Ron's eyes widen as he caught a glimpse of the social worker as she entered the café.

He called out to her, "Josephina, over here."

Emily turned to see the newest lunch guest make her way across the diner. Instead of the usual briefcase, sensible shoes, and dowdy dress, Mrs. Garcia wore a Rolling Stones T-shirt, dark denim jeans, and bright-red sandals. Her shiny black hair was pulled back into a ponytail. She wore thick tortoiseshell-framed glasses and carried a red leather attaché.

She greeted Father Ron and Miki before turning to Emily. Her olive-green eyes sparkled as she said, "Hi, Emily, I'm Josephina Garcia. Father Ron has told me a lot about you and your situation. My goodness, girl, you've been through a lot, haven't you?"

Emily shrugged.

Mrs. Garcia wiggled into the booth next to Father Ron. "I'm starved, and the good Padre promised me lunch. I didn't know the church gave you a raise, Ron. Let's eat before he changes his mind and sticks me with the bill."

Father Ron signaled to the waitress. Looking over the menu, Emily decided on the fried chicken special. It reminded her of the last time she and Dad had a meal together.

"Tell me a little about yourself, Emily." Mrs. Garcia opened the attaché, and pulled out a thin file folder, revealing a pile of forms.

"What do you want to know?" Emily's heart began to beat faster, and her face flushed.

"Let's start with your name." Mrs. Garcia dug in her purse for a pen.

"Emily."

"That much I know. Emily what?"

"Just Emily."

"Look, Just Emily, I can't help you if you don't cooperate."

Emily folded her arms and sat back in the booth. "Emily Freakin' Anderson."

"Okay, Emily Freakin' Anderson, tell me your story. How did you end up on the streets?"

Emily looked at Miki.

Miki nodded her head. "It's okay. Josephina is here to help. And she can't unless you tell her the whole story."

Emily sat up straight, wondering how much she could put her faith in these people.

Mrs. Garcia's eyes softened as she closed the file folder and laid down her pen. "No formal forms, just you and me. Tell me what happened."

Emily took a breath. Just as she was about to speak, the waitress arrived with their meals.

Emily sliced off a hunk of chicken while gathering her thoughts. She wasn't sure where to begin and how much to tell. She watched Father Ron bite into his sandwich. Again, Miki gave her a silent nod of reassurance. So she started at the beginning, leaving out the secrets.

When she finished, Josephina raised her eyebrows and sighed. "You've been out of school how long?"

"Two years," Emily said.

"How did you do it? How did you survive that long?"

"Dad and I kept on the move. When he worked, I hid out in libraries or a McDonald's, or I would go to stores and watch TV. Sometimes I just stayed in the car. I read. I kept a journal."

"You know you are going to have to return to school," Josefina said.

Emily squirmed in her seat. "No way. I've made it this far. I don't need school."

"It's the law. You must stay in school until you're sixteen."

"I'll be sixteen soon. Why can't I just work?"

"You need an education if you are going to make it in this world, Emily," Father Ron said. "You can live with Miki and Da-Shawn on a temporary basis. Josephina assures us that it can be arranged through DFS."

"Whoa, when was all this decided?" Emily frowned and looked at Miki.

"We didn't want to tell you until we were sure," Miki said.

"Tell me what?"

"Da-Shawn and I want you to live with us until your dad can take care of you. We spoke to Father Ron and Josephina before this meeting."

"Why didn't anyone freakin' ask me? I can damn well take care of myself. I don't need any—"

"Sleeping in a church and eating at a soup kitchen is no way to take care of yourself." Father Ron looked at Emily with kind eyes. "We've also spoken to the guidance counselor at the local high school. Because of your age, they're able to put you in the tenth grade. Or if you want, you can attend virtual school."

"Wait just one minute. You want me to live with Miki, go to school, and I have nothing to say about it?"

"Okay," Miki said, "tell us what you think."

Emily ran her fingers through her hair. "I appreciate you letting me crash at your place. I totally do, but why can't I just work until I can afford my own apartment? I won't be there long."

"Do you have any idea how much it costs to live on your own?" Miki put her hand over Emily's. "Da-Shawn and I want you to stay with us. You fill a spot in our hearts that has been empty for so long. You can continue to work on weekends and some nights after school. And if you decide to attend virtual school, I can set up a computer in the back room for you."

Not used to kindness, Emily felt unwanted tears pool in the corners of her eyes. She watched one teardrop land on the plastic seat and roll to the floor. She squeezed her eyes together in an attempt to stop them and prayed. *Oh, God, please, not now. I can't cry now.*

She wanted to trust, to hope, but what good had it done her in the past? Mom had abandoned her. Dad couldn't overcome his taste for drugs.

Emily felt trapped and couldn't believe the next thing that came out of her mouth. "Okay."

Miki's voice was a whisper. "Okay. Does that mean you'll stay with me and Da-Shawn?"

"Do I have a choice?"

Miki looked down at her hands. "There's always a choice in life."

"I'll get the paperwork started, Miki," Josephina said.

"Is that all there is to it?" Emily asked.

"Paperwork and then an order from a judge, but it will be fine," Josephina assured her.

"What if the judge doesn't agree? What if I'm put in a foster home?" Emily rubbed her arms. She realized she was holding her breath, so she let it out.

"I know people in high places. It'll be a piece of cake," Josephina said.

"And I know people in higher places," Father Ron added.

Just then, the waitress brought over four pieces of chocolate cake and plunked them down in front of the group. "Looks like you're celebrating something good." The waitress set the bill by Father Ron.

That night, before going to sleep, Emily opened her journal.

> Today was a scary day. This morning I freaked when I saw a man that looked like that whacked perv who tried to attack me. He was going to Miki's house to fix the washing machine. He had a scary tattoo on his arm just like the perv. Then the psycho lady from the shelter showed up at work. She has a name—Alice, but I still like to think of her as Tin Lady. She says all sorts of creepy stuff to me. Scares the living crap out of me. OMG—I almost got caught stealing money from Miki. How stupid was that? I could end up in Juvie. What's that saying? Something about the apple not falling too far from the tree. Dad and me—jailbirds.
>
> If the day couldn't get any worse, I now have a social worker looking into my life. She's pretty

cool, but I'm not so sure I trust her. She's trying
to get Miki and Da-Shawn as my guardians
until Dad gets out of jail. I have to go to court—
not sure what happens then. The worst is going
to be school. Now there's a place I really want to
avoid. Sixteen can't come too soon.

Before putting away her journal, she thumbed
through her sketches. She stopped at a blank page and
started to draw a woman in a business suit.

A tap on the door made her slam it shut and quickly
slip it under her pillow.

"Just came to say good night," Miki said, peering
around the door.

"Come in." Emily adjusted the pillow.

"Are you okay with everything that happened
today?" Miki asked.

Emily ran her fingers through her hair. "Yeah.
It's good."

"I brought you a present." Miki handed Emily
a small bronze dragon. "Put this at the window.
For protection."

Emily's fingers touched the open mouth of the
dragon, feeling the sharpness of its teeth. She leaned
over and placed it on the ledge of the window. "You say
it'll protect me. From what?"

"From any dangers that come into your life,"
Miki said.

"I wish I had something like this when…"

"When what?" Miki asked.

Emily shrugged. "Just when." Then she added,
"Thanks."

Miki slipped out of the room, and Emily withdrew the journal from under her pillow. She opened it and picked up a pencil. The sketch of a dragon took shape on the page. Then a man—his body on fire from the breath of the dragon.

Courage to change the things I can…

Emily rubbed her sweaty hands on her jeans as she opened the closet door to choose an outfit for court. She and Miki had gone shopping the day before and found three. She lifted out the blue-checkered dress and tried it on one more time. She added the denim jacket and strappy sandals. Twirling before the mirror, she felt cool and trendy.

The ride to court took forever. She felt the tickle of a butterfly in her stomach when she saw the looming edifice of the courthouse.

"What if he sends me away?" She looked up to see Da-Shawn's smoky eyes watching her from the rearview mirror.

"Don't bring worry on yourself, Em. Everything will work out. You'll see," he said.

"Da-Shawn's right. Everything will be okay," Miki added.

Emily couldn't stop wringing her hands.

CHAPTER 13

Groups of people stood on the grass at the far end of the courthouse, smoking cigarettes and chatting. Two scraggly dogs roamed in search of food under benches that were scattered around a gazebo. One woman with teased orange hair held out part of a sandwich. The larger of the two dogs snatched it from her hand. The smaller dog moved on to the next person in hopes of getting a morsel. Emily was surprised when she looked up to see Tin Lady pushing her precious shopping cart along the sidewalk.

As the trio approached, Miki smiled and greeted her. "Good morning, Alice. What brings you here?"

Tin Lady gazed at Emily before saying, "Be careful. Very, very careful."

As they passed by, Emily turned to Miki. "That lady creeps me out."

Miki nodded, and Da-Shawn added, "It's her illness. I wouldn't put too much stock in her warning."

Uniformed officers opened the large glass doors to the building. People poured through and stood in a line, like visitors waiting for a ride at Disney World. Emily, Da-Shawn, and Miki joined the queue. Emily felt a shiver run through her as she tried to shake off Alice's admonition.

"Why do we have to stand in line?" Emily craned her neck to see where this was leading.

"Just like the airport, we have to go through security," Miki explained.

"That's so stupid." Emily wiped her hands on her jeans again as the line snaked around the corner.

When they reached the checkpoint, Emily placed her backpack on a conveyer belt and walked through the metal detector. She turned to see Da-Shawn emptying his pockets of change, keys, and gum. Miki followed, placing her purse on the conveyer belt.

After being cleared, they stopped at the directory and saw that the juvenile court was on the ninth floor, room 913. They stepped into the crowded elevator. The stench of grimy sweat assaulted Emily. She turned her head slightly, picking up a familiar odor.

No one spoke as the elevator inched up floor by floor, stopping only to let people move in and out.

Suddenly, a hand touched her shoulder, sending a wave of fear up her spine.

The unpleasant smell. The touch. Then the raspy voice. "Long time no see, little girl. What brings you here?"

Emily turned to see Frank. Smiling, tilting his head, reaching out to her.

"Don't touch me, jerk," Emily whispered through clenched teeth.

"Now, is that the way to treat an old friend?" His lips were so close to her ear she could feel his breath on her neck.

The doors opened. Emily pushed through the throng of people, bolted from the elevator, and started to run. Before the doors closed, she heard Miki call out, "Em, where are you going?"

"I'm taking the stairs!" But the elevator doors closed before the words could reach Miki.

When Emily arrived at the ninth floor, she saw Da-Shawn and Miki standing in the hallway with Josephina.

"What was that all about?" Miki frowned as Emily rounded the corner.

Breathless and shaking, Emily said, "I'm a bit claustrophobic. That elevator was too crowded. I couldn't breathe."

Josephina was dressed in a navy-blue suit and carrying a black leather briefcase. Her power suit, she explained, as she opened the large oak doors. "Are you ready?"

The courtroom held a throng of people. The sound of voices bounced off the walls as feelings of apprehension dominated the room. Sensory overload bore down on Emily as she took in the foreign scene and tried to shake off the elevator experience.

Three boys huddled on pew-like benches in the front row. One sat with his arms resting on his knees, a small dragon tattoo snaking around the nape of his neck. The other two leaned back, arms crossed, defiant sneers masking fear.

A young couple, holding a baby dressed in green overalls and a blue-and-green-striped shirt, sat across from the tattooed boys. The couple smiled as the baby laughed and bounced on his father's knee.

Josephina directed them to the second row. Emily sat next to a girl in a denim miniskirt and low-cut tank top who was making irritating snapping sounds with her gum. She held an iPod in one hand, and her head swayed to an indiscernible tune.

"So what are you here for?" Denim Girl whispered as she removed the buds from her ears.

"I'm getting a guardian," Emily said.

Snap, snap. She spoke around her gum, "I got picked up for possession. My lawyer said he could get me off."

Emily frowned. "Where are your mom and dad?"

Denim Girl turned around and pointed. "Back there. My mom's the prissy, uptight woman with the flowered dress, and the nerd beside her is my stepdad. They're too freakin' embarrassed to sit by me."

Before Emily could look, she heard, "All rise. The Honorable Judge George Watson presiding." She watched the small man in black robes sit and bang his gavel. He looked over his tiny reading glasses at the gallery and then down at a piece of paper in front of him.

"I see we have an adoption." The judge looked at the young couple and grinned. "Bailiff, call the first case."

The bailiff looked at the young couple as he called out their name.

Emily couldn't help but smile to herself as the two kissed before rising.

When the adoption was finalized, Emily heard her name called. She, Miki, Da-Shawn, and Josephina walked through the small wooden gate that separated them from the tattooed boys and Denim Girl. They approached the bench and stood before the judge.

Emily hoped no one would see her trembling hands. She watched the shiny buttons on her dress dance to the rhythm of her heartbeat. The judge read over a stack of papers before looking at her. He smiled. When he spoke, Emily couldn't hear him. She felt lightheaded.

Stay focused, she told herself. She forced herself to look at the judge. His black robe was a blur, and she heard buzzing all around as if she was sitting in a cell of a honeybee hive.

Emily shook her head as Josephina spoke. "Yes, Your Honor, I found the house to be in excellent…"

The buzzing grew louder.

"Your paperwork is in order…" The judge was leafing through a file, but the bees took flight and landed in Emily's stomach.

Focus, come on, focus.

She could hear Miki and DaShawn. "We will…"

"So ordered…"

The room began to spin. A loud rap of the gavel jolted Emily out of the fog, but her legs gave out.

Da-Shawn's strong arms caught her.

Miki shouted, "We need water!"

Realizing she had fainted, Emily's face reddened. "I'm good." She took a deep breath and felt her heartbeat slow down.

"I told you to eat breakfast, girl," said Da-Shawn, leading her to a chair. Miki sat down beside her.

The judge was standing now. "Is everyone okay?"

"She just needs little water." Da-Shawn looked at the judge. "I think she's dehydrated and a little shaky from all the excitement."

"Is it over?" Emily asked.

"Congratulations. It's over." Josephina shook Da-Shawn's hand and hugged Miki. "Let's go outside and go over the judge's orders before you leave."

As they walked up the aisle, Emily heard the bailiff call, "Samantha White." She watched Denim Girl rise, tuck her iPod into her purse, and swagger toward the bench. The woman in the floral dress blew her nose and followed Denim Girl. The nerdy man sat motionless.

Emily reached for Miki's hand. Da-Shawn put his arm around her shoulders as they walked through the courtroom doors.

Josephina led them to a small room across the hall. They sat at a large polished wooden table. Emily listened as Josephina explained the terms of the guardianship. She looked at Emily and said, "You will need to register at the local high school tomorrow."

"Impossible!" Emily ran her fingers through her hair. "I haven't been to school in two years. I don't even know how to do school—sit in a desk, make friends. Can't I just work for Miki?"

"You're too young," Miki said. "Don't worry. Da-Shawn and I are here to help you through this."

Emily took a deep breath and let it out slowly as she pondered the future.

That night, wrapped in a soft white blanket, she sat in bed and opened her journal.

> OMG, today was surreal. Before even going to court I ran into that stinkin' perv, Frank, in the elevator. He touched me and nearly scared the crap out of me. I thought he was dead! I should have told Miki about him, but just wanted it to go away. My life is crazy-wild. I passed out in court...how lame is that? The place was filled with some gnarly people. I feel totally unhinged. Tomorrow I have to start school. OMG—school! I haven't the first clue about what to do, what to wear, how to act. I don't understand why I can't just work. I'll be sixteen soon and will drop out.

She bit the end of the pencil before drawing a picture of three boys, one of them sporting a dragon tattoo. She added a girl in a denim miniskirt and then ripped the page out of the journal, wadded it up, and threw it across the room.

CHAPTER 14

Emily knew she was going to puke. Her stomach hurt, her hands shook, and she couldn't keep her knees from shaking.

She looked up, watched Miki turn the steering wheel, and pull into the space marked Visitors. School— an experience in disaster. How would she ever survive?

Miki put her hand on Emily's shoulder. "Are you ready?"

Emily shrugged. "Do I have a choice?" She opened the door and slipped out of the car.

The massive brick building stood three stories high. As they walked toward the entrance, Emily hesitated and looked at Miki. "Maybe I should go the virtual route. I'm not so sure of this."

"Give it a try. If it doesn't work out, we can always explore other options," Miki said. They stepped through the door to a rush of teens breezing through the hallways. Emily jumped when a boy in a Gap shirt slammed a locker door as she passed. She watched a girl rush by, applying lipstick. Emily touched her dry lips. She never wore makeup. It was a luxury. Food, gas, and clean clothes—they were the necessities when you were on the road.

Miki stopped one girl to ask for directions to the office. "Two doors down on your right."

"You would think I'd remember. After all, it's only been three years since I've walked through these halls." Miki stepped aside to let a group of boys pass and then gasped. "Oh no. No!"

Emily turned to see Miki's ashen face, her eyes fixed on a bulletin board beside them. Large red letters made out of construction paper spelled out *SADD* at the top. Four framed pictures of smiling young faces surrounded it. Joy's portrait stood out, with the dates of her birth and death etched on a bronze nameplate.

"I didn't think it would be this hard to come back here," Miki whispered.

Emily stood in silence. She couldn't summon words of comfort.

When they arrived at the office, Emily watched a gray-haired lady scamper from behind her protective counter and hug Miki. "How are you, Mrs. Jarrell?"

Miki returned the hug and said, "As well as can be expected, Miriam. I've come to enroll Emily Anderson, but I'd like to see Mrs. Allen first."

"She's expecting you. Sit down. I'll let her know you're here." The gray-haired lady returned to her station behind the counter and picked up the phone.

A minute later, a small woman holding an armful of file folders approached them. "Mrs. Jarrell, it's so good to see you." She looked at Emily and extended her hand. "You must be Emily. I'm Mrs. Allen, the guidance counselor." She shook Emily's hand and then turned back to Miki. "Mrs. Jarrell, thank you for the phone call. It's been a long time. How are you doing?"

"I'm good." Miki smiled at Mrs. Allen. "But seeing Joy's picture on the SADD bulletin board brought back some not-so-good memories."

"We have a large number of our students in the club. In fact, an officer from the local police department is coming over today to give a lecture on the dangers of texting while driving." Mrs. Allen returned Miki's smile. "Come into my office so I can help Emily get registered."

Emily sat on the overstuffed sofa that graced one corner. The sweet scent of lavender filled the air. She looked at the lava lamp that gave the room a soft, comforting glow. Small purple bubbles rose and fell inside it like the ups and downs of her life. She gazed at the large poster that covered the wall behind her counselor's desk. The saying "Obstacles are things a person sees when he takes his eyes off the goal" jumped out at her. Brass words surrounded the rest of the walls—*Believe*, *Hope*, and *Imagine*.

Mrs. Allen took a seat in the chair across from her. "I've spoken to Mrs. Garcia about your circumstances, Emily. You've been through quite an ordeal. You know that you can come to me with any questions or problems."

Emily nodded.

"When we spoke, you indicated that you would put her in the tenth grade because of her age," Miki said. "What if she can't..." Miki hesitated and then continued, "What if she finds it too difficult?"

"That's a possibility, but I can assure you that I'm here to help. I've talked to all of Emily's teachers, and they know the circumstances. She will come to me twice a week after school to go over any problems she may encounter. How does that sound to you, Emily?"

Emily sat with her hands folded in her lap. She nodded again and then looked directly at Mrs. Allen. "That sounds good. I've read a lot while I was on my own. I'm good at drawing."

How lame do I sound? Maybe I should tell her that I can fight off a perv, or make a McDonald's happy meal last two days.

Mrs. Allen smiled and handed Emily her schedule. "Take a look at these classes. I managed to get you into an art class. I think you will fit in nicely. Come on, we're in second period. Let me show you around and then I can walk you to your classroom."

As they traversed the halls, they passed a girl with a neatly tied braid falling halfway down her back, wearing a brick-red T-shirt with the word *Gap* running down the side and jeans tattered at the knee. "Ava." Mrs. Allen stopped. "Come over here. There's someone I want you to meet.

Emily watched the girl turn and smile. "Hi, Mrs. Allen."

"Ava, this is Emily Anderson. It's her first day here, and you have some classes with her. Emily, this is Ava Dawson."

Emily adjusted her backpack and said, "Hi."

Ava smiled. "Hi, Emily. Welcome to Braxton High."

Gotta be a cheerleader. 'Welcome to Braxton High.'
How freakin' perky.

"Could you escort her around today and introduce her to some of your friends? In fact, you both have second period together. Will you walk her to class?" Mrs. Allen asked.

"Sure, Mrs. Allen. Come on, Emily. Let me see your schedule."

Emily felt butterflies flutter in her stomach. *Great, a preppie goodie-goodie. This is going to be harder than I thought.*

Emily handed her schedule to Ava as they started toward a classroom located at the end of the hall.

"Good luck, Emily," Mrs. Allen called out. "I know you will like it here."

Ava said, "She's right, you know. This is a good school. Where'd you go before here?"

Where'd I go before here? Let me think. Should I tell her Toyota U?

"A high school in Houston. My dad just got sent to Afghanistan," Emily lied. "So I'm staying with my aunt, Miki."

"Afghanistan. Wow your dad's a solider? I'll bet you miss him."

"Yeah. I'm used to it, you know," she continued. "This is his second tour."

Emily discovered that she was in four of Ava's classes. At least she knew someone even if the perkiness was irritating.

They ate lunch together, and Ava introduced her to other girls in her group—all cheerleaders. Rah, rah.

After being on the streets for two years, Emily found the routine of school as confining as the backseat of her previous home. But survival meant enduring a few months until she was sixteen and could quit.

That night, Emily opened her journal.

> Started school today. Me and school—go figure. I feel like an alien that crashed into a foreign planet. After just one day of cramming myself into desks, I kind of know how Dad feels locked up in jail.

> The guidance counselor made some girl show me around. She was pretty nice, but such a goodie-goodie. She introduced me to some of her friends. Talk about awkward—I haven't had a friend since I was...let me see, 10 years old. Sixteen can't come soon enough.

Before closing her journal, Emily decided to design some T-shirts and jeans for the Gap's new catalog.

CHAPTER 15

Friday. Art. Last period. Emily wrinkled her nose as she entered the room. The smell of paint mixed with that of sharpened pencils hung over the room. The sound of footsteps hurrying to tables, the buzz of friends talking, and the shuffling of papers echoed off the walls. Emily gazed out the window at the mid-October sky. She watched a maple leaf break free, dancing downward on invisible breezes.

For the past six weeks, Emily worked furiously to catch up to her classmates. Mrs. Allen met with her every Monday and Wednesday after school for the first month. Adjusting to the high school routine was easier than Emily thought it would be. Ava became her best friend and included her with the other girls in her group.

Mrs. Tate clapped her hands to silence the class. Everyone settled down as they watched her turn toward the board and write in large letters, "Art Fair, December 1–3," and underneath, in smaller letters, "Artwork due November 21."

"As you all know, the tenth grade is responsible for the art fair this year. We are raising money to purchase blankets for St. Gerard's, our local homeless shelter."

Emily leaned back in her seat. She knew just what she would do. Tucked away between the pages of her journal were six pencil drawings of coordinated outfits and one formal gown.

At lunch, she and Ava discussed their ideas for the fair.

"You're lucky," Ava said. "You have your designs already started. I'm not sure what to do. I was thinking about something in clay."

"Clay's good. You know, I've been drawing for a while now. My dad's a good artist. I take after him." Emily ran her fingers through her hair as she looked at the tray before her.

"Have you heard from your dad yet?" Ava asked.

"No. He's on some secret mission." A lie. "But I've written him." Not a lie.

"Has he written you back?"

"No. Not yet. It takes a while for my letters to get to him." Emily poked at the mac and cheese that was the day's special. "Yuck, they call this food?"

"Why don't you come over to my place tonight?" Ava said. "My mom's fixing cheeseburgers. And you can meet my brother, Eli. You'll like him."

"Can't. It's pizza night with my aunt and my uncle."

Sitting at a table draped in a red-and-white-checkered plastic tablecloth, Da-Shawn wrinkled his forehead. "What do you mean by the veggie special, girl? Pepperoni is the only way to eat pizza. Since when have you gotten on this vegan kick?"

"Pepperoni is so bad for you, Da-Shawn." Emily shook her finger at him and laughed. "You should know better. And you call yourself a nurse?"

Da-Shawn puffed out his chest. "Do as I say, not as I eat. That's my motto."

Miki rolled her eyes. "Cut it out, you two. Here comes our dinner."

The earthy smell of basil mixed with tangy tomato sauce greeted them as the waiter set two large pizzas down at their table. Da-Shawn rubbed his hands together. "Now there's a meal fit for a king."

"You're going to look like Henry VIII if you keep eating like that," Emily chided him.

A couple at the next table laughed. "We don't mean to eavesdrop, but it's refreshing to see a family having so much fun."

A family, Emily thought. A family. The image warmed her more than the hot cheese oozing from the pizza.

That night, when the house was quiet, Emily jumped into bed and grabbed her journal. She dog-eared the pages of designs that she would submit for the art fair. Picking up a pencil, she wrote,

> Had pizza tonight with Miki and Da-Shawn. This family thing is fun. Even the school thing is okay—especially art. I hate algebra though—what crazy person invented that horrid subject? Da-Shawn tries to explain it to me, but I think it has changed since he was in school. Work is good. I like the money. But dusting shelves can get so totally boring. Got to help Miki unpack tomorrow.

Before closing her journal, Emily drew pictures of vases and bowls.

Maybe I'll show these to Ava, she thought before switching off the bedside light.

CHAPTER 16

"We've got a lot of unpacking to do." Miki stood with her hands on her hips, looking over the boxes that were delivered on Friday. "Look at this mess. I'm glad you can help out today. I have errands to run."

Emily took the box cutter away from Miki. "Go. I can totally take care of the store and stack the shelves."

"What about homework?"

"It's the weekend, Miki. I can do it tomorrow. I'm going to Ava's house. We're working on a science project together." Emily sliced open a box sitting in the corner.

"Sunday, after church," Miki reminded her.

Emily rolled her eyes. "After church. You and Father Ron aren't going to leave me alone, are you?"

"Just helping you keep body and soul together." Miki hugged her and continued, "By the way, I have a workman coming in to repair that broken shelf in back. If I'm not back in time, will you show him what to do?" Miki lifted the shelf and set it against the wall.

"Yeah. Will you be long?"

"I'm meeting Da-Shawn for lunch, so I'll be gone a couple of hours. Will you be okay?"

"I can totally handle things here. Take your time."

"Want me to bring you back anything?"

"Something sweet? Chocolate. I'm so wanting candy."

Emily watched Miki slip out the back door. She turned to the boxes that had been delivered the day before and picked up the box cutter. The first box contained a dozen bronze dragons. Just as she was about to unload them, she heard the tinkling of the bell.

Emily put down the cutters and parted the curtain that separated the back room from the store. A burly man stood by the cash register. "Can I help you?" she said.

Her eyes flew open at the sight of his arm and the tattoo of the evil dragon. She started to shake.

"Well, well, well. Hello, little girl." Frank's crooked smile took on a malevolent appearance.

"What are you doing here, you perv?" Emily shouted.

"Now, is that any way to treat an old friend?" Frank took a step closer.

"Get out before I call the police." Emily turned and walked toward the phone.

"No can do. Your boss called me to fix a shelf. Got work to do."

"Not today. Get out or I'll scream." Emily ran into the back room, and grabbed the box cutter.

Frank stepped in and said, "Cozy little space you have here."

"Come any closer and I'll—"

"You'll what?" Frank challenged.

The *ding* of the bell alerted them that someone else had entered the store. Neither moved. Frank was the first to step out of the back room. "So what's the boss want?"

Emily looked up to see Alice struggling to open the front door. Her crowded cart stood on the sidewalk by the window. "The shelf leaning against the back wall needs to be mounted."

Frank looked over the shelf. "Gotta get some tools from my truck. Be back, little girl."

Emily watched as Frank held the door open for Alice and then walked to his truck.

"Alice, I have a cinnamon roll for you." Emily moved to the counter, still grasping the box cutters. She reached for the cinnamon roll and handed it to Alice.

Alice's dark, brooding eyes never left the door as she reached for the bun. "He's a bad one."

Emily nodded. "Stay. I'll fix you some tea. It'll go good with the roll."

"Got some place to be."

Emily grabbed Alice's arm and pleaded, "Just for a little bit. Until the bad man is gone."

Alice nodded and sat in the antique yoke-back chair near the main aisle of the store.

Frank returned and sauntered over to the broken shelf. Emily parked herself on a bench next to Alice.

"So, where's my tea?" Alice's eyes never left Frank.

"Ohmigosh, I forgot." Emily stood, tightened her grip on the box cutter, and went into the back room to start the water. When she heard the whistling of the kettle, she dropped two tea bags into the YiXing teapot. The sound of the banging hammer gave her some relief.

She returned to the front of the store and sat next to Alice. Frank turned and said, "Got something for me, little girl?"

"They're watching you," Alice said. Her eyes narrowed as she stared at Frank.

"Who's watching me, freaky lady?" Frank glared at Alice.

Alice glowered back. Frank turned and lifted the shelf, securing it in place.

Alice and Emily sat close to each other. Neither of them talked as they sipped their tea and watched Frank.

After Frank had put the last of his tools in his belt, he turned and walked up to Emily. He stood so close the stench of his stale sweat made her back away. "Where's my check?" Frank held out his hand.

Emily walked into the back room, Frank close behind her.

Tin Lady said, "You stay with me."

Frank turned. "Shut up, freak."

Emily stopped. "You'll get your check. Wait out here."

Frank folded his arms, jutted his chin out, and said, "Hurry. Time's money."

After tucking the check in his shirt pocket, he opened the door and left. Alice and Emily watched him amble toward his truck, stop, and look at the shopping cart. With one sweep of his large, muscular arm, he pushed it, scattering all of Alice's possessions on the sidewalk.

Alice let out a scream so loud it echoed through the entire store. She raced out the door and charged at

Frank like a mother bear protecting her cub. He grabbed a shovel from the back of the pickup and flew at Alice. With an arcing motion, the shovel made contact with Alice's head. Emily rushed outside just in time to watch Alice fall onto the street. She heard someone yell, "Call 911." The exhaust from the pickup rose up to assault her as Frank sped away.

A crowd gathered around the two. Someone handed Emily a towel. As she pressed it to Alice's bleeding head, she heard the scream of a siren in the distance. "Hurry. Hurry."

A stranger touched Emily's shoulder. "Let me help you."

"No, I can't let her go." Emily peered through the crowd. "Where's that ambulance? She's gonna die."

Amid the screech of brakes, the din of the siren, the spinning lights, and the rush of paramedics Emily was finally able to let go of Alice.

"Is she going to be all right?" Emily held Alice's hand as the paramedics examined the wound on her head.

"We have to get this foil off her." A paramedic held blood-soaked gauze in one gloved hand while trying to cut through the foil with the other.

Emily started to shake, remembering the day her brother lay crumpled on the street, blood streaming from his head. "It's my fault. She was trying to help me."

"Are you her daughter?" A policeman had entered the scene with a small notebook in hand.

"No. Just a friend."

"How about family? Do you know someone we can contact?"

"I don't think she has any. She's homeless."

The policeman closed his notebook and shook his head.

They heard the paramedic call out, "Let's get her on the stretcher and to the hospital. She's in bad shape."

Emily stood on the street, watching the ambulance until it turned the corner, the siren fading. She jumped when she felt a hand on her shoulder. "What in the world happened here? Are you okay?" She turned to see Miki trembling.

"Oh, Miki." Emily covered her face with her hands and began to sob.

Miki held on to Emily. Both were shaking. "I thought you'd been hit by a car. When I saw all the blood...thoughts of Joy came flooding back. I couldn't lose another daughter."

Emily shook her head. "No, it's Alice. She's hurt real bad. We need to get to the hospital."

"Take a deep breath first, and tell me what happened." Miki stepped back to make sure Emily wasn't hurt.

"I had asked her to stay with me while the workman fixed the shelf."

"I don't understand."

Emily took a deep breath. She looked at Miki. "I don't even know where to begin."

"The beginning. Start at the beginning and tell me what's so bad that you've kept it hidden."

"It started this summer when Dad found a job with a guy named Frank. The night before my dad went to jail, he left me alone in the car. I didn't mind. He did this a lot. But that night, Frank must have followed us from the restaurant and…"

Miki stood with her arms crossed. "Go on. What happened?"

Emily opened her mouth, but the words were too vile, too frightening to say. Emily started to shake as she met Miki's gentle eyes.

"It's okay. You can tell me. Nothing can be that bad."

"This is," Emily said. "He tried to rape me."

Miki's mouth dropped open. "You mean the workman I hired had assaulted you?"

Emily nodded and looked down.

"We have to notify the police." Miki took hold of Emily's hand. "We can't have a man like that around here."

"But what about Alice? It's my fault she's hurt. Just like when Danny died. I should have done something."

"What could you have done?" Miki took Emily's hand.

Emily shrugged her shoulders. "Will I ever forget? Reminders of that day when he died live deep within me."

"You have to forgive yourself, Em. It wasn't your fault. It was an accident."

Emily looked at Miki. "What about you? Have been able to forgive yourself about Joy's accident?"

Miki shook her head and whispered, "No."

CHAPTER 17

The antiseptic smell of alcohol and bleach mixed with an undertone of sickness hung over Alice's room. The groaning from the curtained area next to her made Emily's flesh crawl as if tiny mites were dancing up and down her arms.

Emily sat on one side of the bed, Miki on the other, when Da-Shawn opened the door and peered in. "Alice is going to be okay. She's got a concussion. We put in ten stitches. It's a miracle she wasn't hurt worse."

"Pray for a miracle—that's what Father Ron told us when he brought the flowers," Emily said.

"I'm glad you were here for her, Da-Shawn," Miki added. "Poor thing has no one."

"She has us." Emily reached into her backpack and pulled out the tattered teddy bear and placed it next to the flowers. A get-well card from the staff of St. Gerard's hung on the wall above the bed.

Instead of tin foil, Alice's head was now wrapped in yards of gauze. "She'll have to keep the bandages on for a while. No tin. I hope she doesn't get too agitated." Da-Shawn checked her stitches to make sure there was no bleeding.

"She's going to go ballistic when she realizes that the tin is gone," Emily said. "I've got an idea. But I need to get my hands on Reynolds Wrap."

"Tell you what, I have an in with the kitchen staff. Next time I pass by, I'll pick you up some," Da-Shawn said.

"What's in that head of yours?" Miki asked as she took hold of Alice's hand.

"You'll see," Emily said.

Later that evening, Da-Shawn was back with an entire roll of Reynolds Wrap. He looked at the sleeping Alice. "She's not awake yet?"

"She needed to be sedated when she realized there was no foil to keep out the radio waves. Emily whispered something to her that seemed to help."

Da-Shawn and Miki watched as Emily fashioned a hat from the foil. She held it up and said, "See, we can put this over the bandages. It won't be too tight. I'll tell her it's a specially designed hospital cap for her protection. What do you think?"

"I think you'll make a good fashion designer." Miki laughed. "Alice will be your first customer."

The sound of heavy boots echoed in the hallway. A tap on the door made Emily jump.

"They're here," Da-Shawn said. "Are you ready?" He looked at Emily.

Emily shrugged. "I guess."

Miki rose to open the door. Two young uniformed police officers stepped into the room.

Emily told them about the recent encounter with Frank, as well as about the horrifying night when he approached her in the car. For too long, she had kept that part of her life hidden, tucked deep within her soul— a secret from another time, when she was another girl. It was an ugly part of her life she wanted— no, needed—to forget. But she discovered that telling someone eased the gnawing pain she had stored up like unwanted trash in an attic.

"Are you sure you can't give us any numbers in the license plate?" one of the officers asked.

"I was too scared. And Alice needed me."

The policeman nodded as he tucked a notepad in his shirt pocket. "Okay. I think we have enough. We'll find him. Don't worry."

As they turned to leave, Emily heard a faint knock at the door. A sliver of light appeared as it opened. "Can I come in?" Ava peeked into the dimly-lit room.

"Ava." Emily rose and hugged her friend.

"Are you okay, Em?" Ava looked at Alice lying in the bed with her tin crown reflecting the light from the small bedside lamp.

Emily took a deep breath. "I'm good now, but it was scary. Come meet my aunt and uncle."

Emily turned to Miki and Da-Shawn and mouthed, *Cover for me. Please.*

Da-Shawn stood and shook Ava's hand while Miki said, "It's finally good to meet you, Ava. Emily's told us so much about you."

Ava smiled and said, "Nice to meet you too." Then she took Emily's hand and led her into the hallway. The two girls walked to a crowded waiting room. A tall, lanky boy sat in one of the chairs, thumbing through a magazine. He stood when they entered.

"My turn to introduce you to someone. My brother drove me here. Come meet him."

Ava's brother was wearing a brown plaid shirt with the sleeves rolled up, exposing the silver watch on his wrist. Straight-legged khakis met polished brown boots. "Eli, this is my friend Emily. Emily, meet my big brother, Eli."

Eli's dark brown eyes sparkled as he extended his hand to greet Emily. His shaggy auburn hair and matching goatee reflected the look of a poet. Emily felt the warmth of his hand as he shook hers.

"You didn't tell me your friend was so pretty." Eli winked at Ava.

Emily felt a flush of heat as her face reddened. She looked down at the floor to avoid his obvious stare.

"Eli's a senior and on the basketball team," Ava continued.

"I hear you had a pretty rough day, Emily. How are you doing? Were you hurt?"

"Not hurt. Totally scared."

"We can't stay long." Ava looked at Eli. "My brother, the star basketball player, has a date."

Emily felt her heart sag. "Oh. Well, thanks for coming."

Emily and Ava hugged. Eli said, "It was nice meeting you."

"Yeah, you too." Emily watched the siblings walk toward the elevator. Before stepping in, Eli turned and waved.

Emily waved back, feeling butterflies flit in her stomach.

When she returned to Alice's room, Da-Shawn was gone. Miki was adjusting Alice's blanket. She turned and said, "What was that all about? Your aunt and uncle?"

Emily ran her fingers through her hair. "Thanks for covering me. I didn't want Ava to, you know, know about me. I told her I was living with my aunt and uncle while my dad was in Afghanistan."

"Be careful. Lies have a way of turning on us."

"I know, but—"

"And, Em, come on, we don't exactly look related. How are you going to get around that one?"

"Maybe I'll tell them you are my step-aunt and step-uncle."

"Hmm. Like I said, lies have a way of turning on us."

That night before going to bed, Emily pulled out her journal and turned to a fresh page.

> A totally unbelievable day. Frank the perv showed up at Miki's store. How weird is that? Was I scared? Totally. But I'm thankful Alice showed up and stayed with me. Things got crazy— wild crazy. Frank the perv almost killed Alice! He dumped over her shopping cart. She went ballistic and attacked him. Then he

attacked her. It was totally bizarre. She's going to be okay. At least that's what Da-Shawn says.

I got caught in my Dad's-in-the-military lie by Miki and Da-Shawn. They were cool about it. No one can know.

I met the cutest boy ever! He's Ava's brother and a real hottie. Too bad he has a girlfriend.

CHAPTER 18

Sunday morning, Emily awoke to the aroma of coffee wafting up the stairs. Her eyes flew open, and she jumped out of bed, grabbing her robe and running downstairs.

Da-Shawn's home!

Her breath coming in gasps, she rounded the counter to see him pouring two cups of coffee. Miki sat at the table with her hands covering her face. "Oh no." Emily started to tremble. "Is it Alice?"

Da-Shawn pulled out a chair, sat, and took a sip of coffee. He looked up, his face haggard. "It's been a long night. Sit down, Em, and let's talk."

Emily sat. She held her breath, waiting for Da-Shawn to speak. "Well? Is she okay."

"It was a rough night," Da-Shawn said. "But don't worry, she's going to heal. It'll just take time. Our biggest worry is what to do when Alice is ready to go home."

"Father Ron is trying to find out if she has relatives," Miki said. "We can't let her out on the streets. And St. Gerard's can't keep her indefinitely."

Emily blew out her breath, and her body sagged. "Poor Alice. We're going to visit her today, aren't we?"

"Of course, but Da-Shawn needs to get some sleep. And we have to go to Mass, and then to the store to finish unpacking. And make sure everything is secure."

Emily walked to the refrigerator and took out the orange juice. She returned to the table and poured herself a glass. That's when she noticed the small gift-wrapped box. She looked up to see both Miki and Da-Shawn smiling.

"What's this?"

"Why don't you open it and see?" Da-Shawn folded his arms and sat back in his chair.

Emily picked up the package and began to unwrap it. She beamed when she saw the contents of the box. "A cell phone! For me?"

"After what happened yesterday, Da-Shawn and I wondered why it took us so long to get you one."

"It's totally cool. Thanks."

"You're welcome. You're part of our family plan. Unlimited everything," Miki said.

"Texting?" Emily asked.

"Text till your thumbs fall off." Da-Shawn laughed. Then he turned to Miki. "Kids today. I wonder if they know the fine art of conversation. Seems like everywhere I am, I see them texting. Even the young doctors."

Emily almost dropped the phone when it vibrated. She looked down to see Ava's name pop up on the screen. She looked up at Miki and Da-Shawn. "So aren't you going to answer it? Push the green button," Da-Shawn instructed.

Emily pushed the On button and said, "Hello?"

"Am I your first caller?" It was Ava.

"Hey. How'd you get my number so fast?"

"I called you last night, but you were asleep. I spoke to your aunt, and she gave me your cell number. Pretty sneaky, huh? So, how are you?"

"Better."

"I have to tell you, you made a big impression on my brother. He couldn't stop talking about you on the way home last night. Can I give him your number?"

Emily felt heat creep into her cheeks.

"He thinks you are totally hot," Ava continued.

"But he just met me."

"That's my brother for you. He's a real charmer. Better be careful."

"What about his girlfriend?" Emily looked up to see Miki and Da-Shawn watching her. "Just a minute, Ava." Emily rose and went into the living room.

"She's a loser. What Eli sees in her is a mystery. She's been in some trouble. Drugs, I think. But whatever it was, she had a good lawyer who got her off."

Emily sighed. "Eli's not into..."

"Drugs? No, he can't. He'd be kicked off the basketball team. And if he wants to go to college, he needs to get a scholarship. My parents have this lame philosophy about us paying for our own college education. They think it will make us stronger—more independent."

Emily heard Miki call from the kitchen. "It's time to get ready for church. You can talk to Ava later."

"Gotta go, Ava." Emily hesitated before saying, "Give Eli my number."

Each time Emily walked through the doors of St. Jude's, the fragrance of the incense, the sight of Jesus hanging on the cross, the flicker of the candles reminded her of how much her life had changed.

People rose as the organ played and the cantor started to sing. Emily turned and saw the altar servers and Father Ron proceed down the aisle.

Father Ron winked in her direction.

She smiled and thanked the Hanging Man for the family that he had given her.

After Mass, Emily, Miki, Da-Shawn, and Father Ron gathered at the local cafe for coffee and doughnuts.

"You still look ragged. Are you sure you got enough sleep?" Miki took a sip of her latte.

"I've gotten by on less." Da-Shawn looked at Father Ron. "Do you think you will have any luck finding Alice's relatives?"

Father Ron nodded. "I have friends."

Emily giggled. "Yeah, yeah, I know. In high places."

"In high places. So, I think if she has family, I'll be able to find them." Father Ron nudged Emily with his elbow. "I see we have a budding comedian here."

"Are you going to the hospital with us?" Miki asked Father Ron.

"No, but I'll make it this evening." He kissed Miki and Emily on the cheek and shook Da-Shawn's hand before leaving.

When they arrived at the hospital, they found Alice propped up in bed and eating lunch. She had one hand on her head, keeping her tin crown in place.

"Is your tin hat slipping?" Emily asked.

"Nope." She chewed for a minute and then continued talking with food in her mouth. "Some government agent stopped by and tried to steal it. But I'm too fast for them. I can smell 'em a mile away."

"Government agent? Is that right?" Da-Shawn asked. "Can't be too careful. Did he say anything?"

"Talked about the bad man." Alice turned to Emily. "Got him good, didn't we?"

"We sure did. How's your head?" Emily noticed the teddy bear's ears peeking out from under the sheets.

"Hurts."

"It'll get better. Can I take a look?" Da-Shawn walked over to Alice.

"No. It's too dangerous in here."

"I have an idea." Emily opened the bedside table and pulled out the roll of Reynolds Wrap. "I'll make a shield that will protect you so Da-Shawn can check you out." She tore off a large sheet and held it up in front of Alice.

Da-Shawn removed the shiny crown and unwrapped the bandages. "Looks good. You're going to heal nicely." He wrapped Alice's head with fresh gauze and replaced the protective crown.

Their visit was cut short when a large nurse bustled in, explaining that they were taking Alice away for some tests.

"I don't need no tests."

Miki tucked Alice's blankets in and said, "It'll be okay, dear. The doctors are here to help you get better."

Da-Shawn peeked at the laptop containing Alice's data before helping her into the wheelchair.

On the way to the elevator, he explained to Miki and Emily what tests Alice would be receiving. "They're taking her for an extensive psychiatric evaluation."

"I'm glad. Perhaps they can find some medication to help her." Miki pushed the Down button, and the elevator doors opened.

Emily hesitated before entering. "You still skittish over elevators?" Da-Shawn held the door for them to enter.

Emily shook her head and stepped in.

CHAPTER 19

The next week in school, Emily's ordeal was all anyone talked about. She was becoming a celebrity. Everyone wanted to sit with her at lunch. And they all wanted details of her nightmare—details she wanted to forget.

She ran into Eli in the hall while she was hurrying to her next class. "Hi, Eli."

"Hey, Emily, where're you going?"

"Algebra. Ick. My worst class. And I have a test."

"Mr. Hunt?"

Emily nodded.

"I'm headed that way. I'll walk with you."

When they reached the door, Eli waved good-bye, and Emily entered the room. She settled in just as the bell rang.

"Okay, ladies and gentlemen. Let's put all your books and papers away." Mr. Hunt adjusted his John Lennon glasses before passing out the test.

Emily felt a film of sweat forming on her hands. She rubbed them on her jeans and picked up a pencil. Da-Shawn had tried to help her study, but the test might as well have been written in Swahili for all she could understand. The snapping of gum across the room distracted her.

"Ms. White, we're all glad to have you back. We missed your snarling face while you were away. Did you forget the rule about gum chewing in my class?"

Emily looked up to see her algebra teacher standing in the back of the room with his hands on his hips, talking to Denim Girl, the person she sat next to in court.

"Sorry, Mr. Hunt." Denim Girl rolled her eyes and shrugged. She took the gum out of her mouth and put it in Mr. Hunt's open hand.

"I guess missing so much school has taken a toll on your memory. Perhaps a stay in detention would help remind you of my classroom rules."

"Whatever." Samantha slouched down in her chair, picked up her pencil, and threw Emily a crooked smile.

Emily ran her fingers through her hair and turned back to the test. *I'm never going to understand algebra,* she thought.

Ava met her in the hallway for lunch. The aroma of turkey mixed with cinnamon and pumpkin filled the school. It was the cafeteria's annual Turkey Feast.

As they pushed their trays through the line Ava said, "I finally finished my clay pots for the art fair."

"I have my sketches ready. I may not understand math, but at least I can do one thing right."

"If those drawings are anything like the ones in your journal, I think you'll win first place." Ava watched the cafeteria lady dish turkey and dressing onto a Styrofoam plate.

Emily and Ava picked up their trays and walked to an empty table.

"Mind if I join you?"

She looked up to see Denim Girl smiling.

"Why aren't you with Eli?" Ava slid over to make room for her.

"He's going to join us." Turning to Emily, Samantha continued, "How'd you do on that stupid algebra test?"

"Lame—totally lame. You?" Emily responded.

"Sucky."

"Hey, sounds like someone needs a tutor. Want me to help?" Eli flashed a grin as he sat next to Samantha.

Emily's heart started beating double time. "Da-Shawn tried to help me, but I am still totally lost. I'll never understand it."

"I had Mr. Hunt last year. I would be more than happy to help you." Eli looked at Emily. "Math is one of my better subjects."

"I bet you would love to tutor her, and more, big brother." Ava punched Eli in the arm.

Samantha wrinkled up her face. "Hey, who's your girlfriend here?"

"I just want to spread my intelligence around." He winked at Emily.

That evening, Father Ron joined the Jarrells for dinner. "I have some news."

"Good or bad?" Da-Shawn asked.

"I think it's good. We've found Alice's family."

Emily put down her fork and looked at Father Ron. "Where? How?"

"Let me start at the beginning. St. Gerard's was going to take Alice in during her recovery, but as we all know, they couldn't keep her indefinitely. They asked the police to comb their missing person's reports. Nothing came up."

Miki passed around a steaming bowl of carrots. "She's been here as long as I can remember. Roaming the streets. No one missed her?"

Father Ron placed a spoonful on his plate. "The police took her fingerprints."

"That couldn't have been easy," Da-Shawn said. "She won't let anyone touch her."

"She struggled and kept screaming about the government trying to get her. But they managed to get one print."

"And?" Emily slathered her potatoes with butter.

"And she's from Chicago. Believe it or not, she was in law enforcement there before her illness. They had her prints on file. She has an older sister who is flying in when she can make arrangements."

"I'm so happy for her," Miki said. "Being alone on the streets is not good for anyone, let alone poor Alice."

Emily nodded. "Totally."

"Oh, Em." Miki covered her mouth with her hand. "I'm so sorry. You, of all people, know how hard it is."

"But I'm here. With you." Emily smiled.

"Um." Da-Shawn hesitated and then continued. "There's a letter for you, Em. It came in the mail today."

"For me?"

Everyone looked up at Da-Shawn. "It's from the county jail. From your dad."

CHAPTER 20

Emily sat on her bed, hands trembling, the plain envelope propped up on the bureau staring at her. The neat handwriting beckoned, but Emily wasn't ready to read it. Instead, she opened her journal and began to write. With her pencil poised, she couldn't move her eyes from the envelope. She closed her journal, walked over to the bureau, and picked up the letter.

She held it, turned it over, and poked her finger into the opening at the edge of the flap.

Emily took a deep breath before she let her finger slide along the top of the envelope, tearing it open. She parted the opening to reveal the folded yellow-lined paper held within.

Reaching inside, she pulled the single sheet of paper out of its cradle.

She unfolded it and laid it on the bed. Dad's handwriting was neat, not the scribbles of a druggie.

For a while, all she could do was stare. What would he say to her? After all this time of silence, what could he say?

Hey, Em,

Thanks for all your letters. I'm so happy to see you are doing well. Miki and Da-Shawn sound like good people. You are lucky. Well, I guess I should say I am lucky.

The last time we were together wasn't one of my finest moments. You see where it landed me. Anyway, I'm sorry for not writing sooner. In fact, I'm sorry for a lot of things. I'm working through step nine in my twelve-step program, and it's time for me to make amends to you and your mom and your brother.

Em, I love you. I know I didn't show it these last few years.

Drops of tears sprinkled the page as Emily read on,

I hope you're not crying.

Emily let out a nervous laugh and wiped away the tears rolling down her cheeks. *Yeah, I know, Dad. Only losers cry.*

Remember when I used to tell you that only losers cry? It's not true, Em. I've done my share of crying here.

I owe you amends for not taking care of you like a real dad should. I'm so, so sorry. The biggest apology I owe you is for blaming you for Danny's accident. Em, it wasn't your fault.

Emily grabbed a Kleenex from the nightstand and blew her nose.

> Your mom and I should never have laid that kind of guilt on you. If it was anyone's fault, it was mine. You were a good sister to Danny. I was beginning to drink then, and a drunk always tries to find someone to blame. How could I be so cruel to you?
>
> Please forgive me, Em. Come visit when you can. I miss you and love you.
>
> Dad
>
> P.S. You'd never guess who is in my cell block. Remember that guy who last hired me? Frank? He's in for assaulting some homeless lady. Looking at five years in the State Pen.

Forgive you? I don't think so. Do you know how hard my life was, Dad? Is now? You and Mom led me to believe I killed Danny. Cruel isn't the half of it, Dad. How about living in a car when other kids had their own rooms, their own beds, and could bathe in a real tub, not a dingy gas station bathroom? How about scrounging for food? Remember that time when you found a KFC bag filled with a half-eaten chicken and you offered it to me? I ran behind the car and puked. How many kids do you think eat out of a Dumpster?

And school—you wouldn't, couldn't, let me go to school. Well, now I am forced to, and I feel so lost and alone and just plain crappy.

Forgive you. No!

Emily wadded the letter up and threw it into the wastebasket.

She heard a rap on the door and Miki whispering, "Are you okay?"

"No."

"Do you want to talk?" Miki opened the door.

Emily shook her head.

"Do you need anything?"

"Yeah, a real dad."

Da-Shawn looked over Miki's shoulder and said, "We're here, Em, when you're ready."

"I know. I just need some time."

After the door closed, Emily opened her journal.

She drew a picture of her dad, her mom, and her brother standing together, holding hands. She drew a large heart around them. Then she wrote,

Dear Dad, Mom, and Danny,

I love you all and miss you so much. Danny, what's it like in heaven? Is Jesus there with you? Mom, where are you? I think about you and worry about you. Why haven't you called me or looked for me? Dad, I love you but forgive? Not yet.

Emily closed the journal and put it in the drawer of her nightstand. She sat thinking about her family. Then she walked over to the wastebasket and retrieved her dad's letter. Smoothing it out, she walked back to her bed and slipped it under her pillow.

Chapter 21

Miki picked Emily up after school on Friday. It had been two weeks since Frank's assault on Alice. "Big day for Alice. She's being released from the hospital. Her sister has come down to take her back to Chicago."

"You know, she creeped me out at first, but I kinda hate to see her go." Emily closed the door and fastened her seatbelt.

"I know what you mean. But her sister has found a nice group home for her. She'll be so much safer and have family close by." Miki started the car and pulled out of the parking space.

When the pair arrived at the hospital, they found Alice sitting up with balloons tied to a wheelchair. The bandages that wrapped her head had disappeared, and she was sporting her tin tiara.

Da-Shawn stopped by before he went on duty. "Well, well, little lady, don't you look ravishing."

Emily watched Alice blush. The new medication that she had been taking was helping her focus. "Da-Shawn, are you flirting with me?"

Everyone laughed.

The door opened. Father Ron stepped in. Behind him stood a tall, slender lady wearing a blue pinstriped shirt and casual jeans. Her short salt-and-pepper hair framed a round face. "Look who I brought with me," Father Ron said. "This is Dory Reynolds, Alice's sister."

Emily watched as Dory walked over to Alice and took her hand. "We've all been so worried about you, Alice," she said. "I can't believe we've finally found you."

"I didn't know I was lost," Alice said.

Dory turned to face the others. "Thank you for taking good care of my sister." She looked at Alice and continued, "Are you ready to go home, honey?"

Alice looked around the room with misty eyes and said, "I don't know."

"You'll be fine, Alice. You've got a lot of old friends in Chicago." Miki kissed her on the cheek.

Emily spotted her teddy bear lying on the pillow of Alice's bed. She walked over and picked it up. "Here, Alice. I want you to have this." She handed the cuddly bear to Alice. "It'll remind you of me."

Alice hugged the bear. "Thank you."

A husky nurse marched into the room. "Time to go, dearie."

"Just a minute." Father Ron walked over to Alice. He made the sign of the cross, placed his hand on her head, and blessed her. Stepping back, he said, "God will take care of you, Alice."

Da-Shawn stood behind the wheelchair and said, "Let me do the honors, sweet lady."

A tear escaped Alice's eye as Emily and Miki both hugged her. They all followed Da-Shawn down the hall as the hospital staff waved good-bye. The elevator doors parted and swallowed the group.

Outside the hospital, everyone hugged again and stepped back as Da-Shawn helped Alice into the car. "You take good care of yourself." He kissed Alice on the cheek before closing the door.

"Bye, Tin Lady," Emily whispered.

"Godspeed," Father Ron murmured.

The group stood and watched the car until it was out of sight.

Emily jumped when her phone vibrated. She pulled it from the pocket of her jeans and saw a message from Eli. She excused herself and walked away. Finding an empty bench, she sat and opened her cell phone to reveal the text.

how r u?

I'm good, Emily texted back.

can u come over 2nite? No homework.

Eli had been texting her a lot lately. She didn't know what it meant. He hadn't asked her out on a date. And when she was over at Ava's house, he ignored her. *What's up with that?*

Not 2 nite. 2 busy.

"Time to go." Miki put her hand on Emily's shoulder.

"Okay." Emily followed Miki away from the hospital.

That evening, after dinner, she put the final touches on her drawings for the art fair.

They were due next Wednesday, the day before Thanksgiving break. Emily decided to call Ava and see how her clay pots were coming along.

Ava answered right away. "Hey, Em, how are you?"

"I'm relieved. Just finished my sketches!"

"Me too. I think my pots may have a chance to win. I hope they sell. St. Gerard's needs the money."

"Miki, Da-Shawn, and I are going to help serve Thanksgiving dinner at the shelter this year. Wanna come?"

"That'd be great. Shall I ask Eli?"

Emily felt warmth spread down to her toes. "Sure, that would be good. What's up with Samantha? I haven't seen them together lately."

"Sounds like someone's fishing for gossip."

Emily felt her face redden and was glad Ava couldn't see her. "He's been texting me a lot."

"Now, that's interesting. He's still seeing Sam. Not sure what's up, though."

CHAPTER 22

On Thanksgiving Day, the holiday smells of sage, nutmeg, and brewing cider hung over the large dining room at St. Gerard's. The sound of dishes clanging, the buzz of people talking, and the shuffle of feet as families passed through the cafeteria-style line filled the room. Turkey with stuffing and all the usual sides beckoned visitors to St. Gerard's.

"Seems weird being on this side of the serving line," Emily whispered to Miki as they piled plates high with food.

She looked up and smiled at a woman with a multicolored scarf wrapped around graying hair. That was when she noticed four children dancing around their mother, who was struggling to settle them on folding chairs at the nearest table. Two women clothed in flowered dresses rose to help the woman with her brood.

Miki smiled. "You've come a long way in the past few months."

In the corner sat the woman in the purple skirt, a shawl around her, nursing the baby she delivered last month.

"See that lady? The one with the baby?" Emily asked.

Miki nodded as she passed a full plate to the next person in line.

Emily continued, "I stood by her pretending she was my mom when I first came here."

Miki put her arm around Emily. "Well, you don't have to pretend anymore."

Emily took a deep breath. She thought back to that night in the Corolla when all she desired was to have her family together. Even though Miki and Da-Shawn filled that void, the longing to see her mother would not go away. *Will I ever spend a Thanksgiving with you, Mom? Do you think of me?*

The hearty sound of laughter jolted her back to the present. She turned to gaze at a table of men. They were all laughing as one man leaned forward, telling stories of his adventures on the street. Men, women, and children—all seated together like one large family on this special day.

Emily scooped a pile of fluffy mashed potatoes and placed them on the plate of a man dressed in a tattered suit. Ava added cranberry sauce. Emily smiled to herself as she listened to Father Ron and Da-Shawn trade jokes as they sliced donated pies at the end of the line.

"This is a great way to spend Thanksgiving," Ava said. "Thanks for asking me to come."

Emily watched Eli carry a tray of food for a gray-haired lady with a cane. "I'm glad Eli came too."

"I bet you are." Ava giggled.

Eli returned and asked, "Em, can you help me? I need to get more chairs from out back. We're crazy busy."

"Ask Da-Shawn," Emily said. "I can't leave my station."

"I can handle it. Go." Ava took the spoon from her.

Emily untied her apron and followed Eli out back, where neatly stacked folding chairs leaned against the wall. "Thanks for coming out. I've wanted to get you alone." Eli handed her two chairs.

Emily took them and started into the cafeteria, not knowing what to say.

After three trips, Eli said, "I think that's enough." He leaned close to Emily. She could smell the musky aroma of his aftershave. "I was wondering if you would like to go to a movie sometime."

Emily blushed. "I thought you were dating Samantha."

"I called it quits. She's too toxic for me. So, what do you think? Would you like to go out someday?"

She hesitated for a moment and then looked into Eli's eyes. "Sure. I have to ask Miki and Da-Shawn first, but it sounds like fun."

Eli took her hand. It felt warm and somehow so right. "You don't mind, do you?"

Emily shook her head as Eli pulled her toward the cafeteria.

She retrieved her spoon from Ava.

"Did I see what I just saw? Was my brother holding your hand?"

Emily grinned. "You saw right."

"What's up with that?"

"He asked me out."

"You're kidding! Are you going to go?"

Emily scooped up mashed potatoes and smiled at the next person in line. "Yeah."

"Sam's going to go ballistic."

"They broke up."

"What! That's news to me. Eli tells me everything."

Emily looked at Ava. "Everything?"

"At least he used to. Be careful. Sam can be mean if she thinks you stole her boyfriend."

"Thanks for the warning. I'm good at taking care of myself."

Da-Shawn walked over to the girls. "It's time to go. Ava, we are all looking forward to having dinner with your family."

Emily hugged Ava. "See you in a few hours."

The Dawsons' house sat back from the road on two manicured acres of land. Tall magnolia trees stood guard along the side while dogwoods lined the drive. A large oak door opened as the group exited the car. "Welcome." Dr. and Mrs. Dawson stood by the front door. Extending his hand to Da-Shawn, he said, "I'm Tom Dawson, and this is my wife, Annie."

"Thank you for having us over. I'm Da-Shawn Jarrell, and this is my wife, Miki."

Everyone turned at the sound of another car entering the driveway. It was Father Ron, who waved as he turned off the engine.

After the introductions, Miki joined Mrs. Dawson in the kitchen to help serve the meal.

A burnt-orange runner ran the length of a table set with elegant china, sterling silver, and tall goblets filled with water. A cornucopia sat in the middle, spilling fruit and red leaves onto the table; and votive candles flickered all around. Everyone sat down.

Father Ron blessed the food.

Excited chatter filled the room as juices flowed from the turkey carved by Dr. Dawson. "Better pay attention, Eli. Someday this will be your job."

"You've got the surgeon's touch, not me," said Eli.

"I'm surprised that we've never met,"Da-Shawn said.

"Hospital's a big place. And I never get to the ER. But I've heard what a good nurse you are, Da-Shawn. If you ever want a change, I could always use you in OR."

"I'll think about it." Da-Shawn picked up his knife and buttered a warm roll.

Miki turned to Mrs. Dawson. "Thank you for having us over. It was a long day at the shelter."

"You're a good family to give up your holiday for others," Mrs. Dawson said. "Thank you for taking Ava and Eli. It's good for them to see that life isn't like this for everyone."

Miki nodded.

Ava looked at Emily. "Did you Skype your dad today?"

Emily watched Miki and Da-Shawn freeze, their forks halfway to their mouths. She tried to appear nonchalant as she answered. "No, he's on some sort of secret mission. Not sure when I can reach him."

"It must be difficult for you, Emily," Dr. Dawson said. "How long has your dad been in the service?"

"I'm not sure. I think I was five when he went in."

"You must have lived in many places. What was your favorite?"

Emily hesitated. *Now what? That little town where Dad and I had to hide from the sheriff because of a bar fight?* "California. I loved San Diego," she said. Out of the corner of her eye, she saw Miki and Da-Shawn raise their eyebrows.

After dinner, Ava and Emily got to work in the kitchen. "You don't mind cleanup detail?" Ava asked.

"Are you kidding? The meal was delicious. It's the least I could do." Emily looked behind her.

"Eli went into his room," Ava said. "He's always disappearing when there's work to do."

They listened to the chatter coming from the living room as Emily handed Ava plates to load in the dishwasher.

"Need any help?"

They turned to see Eli standing in the doorway to the kitchen, with his hands in his pockets.

"We're almost done, big brother. You should have waited ten minutes more," Ava said.

Eli grabbed Emily's hand and said, "Get your coat. Let's go for a walk, and I'll show you around."

Emily looked at Ava, who nodded her approval. "I can finish up. You and Eli go."

The cool evening breeze scattered the few fallen leaves left on the sidewalk. Emily shivered as they ambled through his neighborhood. She gazed at elegant houses worthy of the term *mansion*.

"Tell me more about your family. You hardly talk about them," Eli said. He put his arm around her shoulders.

"Not much to say. My mom died when I was seven, and I travelled a lot because of my dad's job." Emily watched Eli glance over at a three-story house that looked more like a castle than a place where one family resided.

He turned to her and said, "You must miss your dad a lot."

Emily took a deep breath. "Yeah." She walked a little farther from him and said, "But Miki and Da-Shawn are awesome."

"Exactly how are they related to you again?"

"My aunt and uncle." Emily looked at Eli and frowned.

"But they're—"

"Oh, because they're different than me?" Emily shuffled through a pile of leaves to collect her thoughts. "They're really my dad's best friends. I've called them Aunt and Uncle since I was little."

Eli nodded. "I get it." Emily shivered. "You're cold. Do you want to go back?"

"I'm kinda tired. And Miki and Da-Shawn will want to get home early."

When they entered the Dawsons' house, Emily saw that Miki and Da-Shawn already had their coats on.

"Where have you two been?" Miki asked.

"Walking off more food than I should have eaten." Eli rubbed his stomach.

"Ready to leave, Em?" Da-Shawn asked.

Emily nodded.

Later that night, Emily threw herself on her bed. "I know, I know."

Miki said, "You can't keep up all this deception. It's going to catch up with you eventually. Then what?"

Da-Shawn stood in the doorway with his arms crossed over his chest. "Miki's right. You are going to have to be up front with Ava and Eli sooner or later."

"Come on. Do you really think they'll be my friends if they knew my dad was a homeless drug addict and in jail? Look at their dad. Look at their house."

"People will find out eventually," Miki said.

"Maybe. But not from me. Not yet."

Miki was silent and then decided to change the subject. "Did your teacher say anything about your sketches for the art fair?"

Emily took a deep breath and ran her fingers through her hair. "Not really. I'm not sure my sketches will win or even sell."

Miki stood up. "Not sure? Em, you have a real talent. I can't wait to see that blue ribbon." Emily watched Miki stop at the door and turn. "Are you ready for tomorrow?"

"I'm not looking forward to it, if that's what you mean. But I promised Dad I would visit."

Miki nodded and closed the door, leaving Emily with only a sliver of moonlight creeping into the room.

She clicked on a light and reached for her journal.

> Except for a stomachache from eating too much, all I have is good news today. I helped

served at St. Gerard's. It was so much better serving than being served. Father Ron always says it's better to give than to receive. Now I know what he means. My family had dinner at Ava's. Her parents are nice, and her brother— ooh la la—is way cool. I so wanted him to kiss me tonight. I've never had a boyfriend. Miki and Da-Shawn think I should tell him the truth about Dad. But I'm totally going to keep that secret to myself. Can you imagine what they would think?

And speaking of Dad, I'm really scared about tomorrow. I promised him I would visit him after Thanksgiving. I've never been in a jail before. It's freaking scaring me.

Emily started to write more, but then decided to sketch instead. She drew a large heart in the middle of the page. In fancy script she wrote Eli's name. She thought about the day and the warm feeling of his hand in hers. She wanted to draw more but yawned and put her head on the pillow. Closing her eyes, she pictured Eli's face. Then she heard a *ding* from her phone. She reached over and pushed a key. The text was from Eli.

Had a great day 2 day.

Emily texted back, *Me 2*. Then she added, *Still want 2 go 2 the movies?*

Eli texted back, *Yes!!!!!!!!!! :)*

CHAPTER 23

Emily closed the door to the silver Altima and looked up at the tall building that housed her dad. "I'm not sure I can do this."

"Have you changed your mind? I can go in with you if it will help," Miki said.

Emily shook her head.

After filling out the necessary forms, they settled into pale-green chairs. Emily picked up a tattered magazine that rested on a table full of scratches. Her trembling legs kept time to the ticking clock that sat askew on one wall.

"Anderson." The echoing of her name and the click of the boots on the stained tile floor made her jump.

"Here." Emily raised her hand and stood to meet the burly guard.

"Your driver's license, ma'am."

Emily dug in her purse and presented her temporary license. The guard looked at it and then up at Emily. Then he handed it back and pointed to a door at the far end of the room. "Thanks. Go stand over there."

Emily joined the queue.

The click of the lock echoed throughout the room, followed by the sliding away of the heavy door. People, like cattle, were herded into the small anteroom. The door slid shut; again, the lock clicked. Everyone stood in silence, thoughts kept secret, known only to them.

A small child clung to a ragged doll. Emily's heart felt heavy; she wondered what it was like for a girl so small to see her dad in a place like this.

No one moved; everyone kept their eyes downcast. Then there was another click—this one louder. The heavy door slid open. Feet shuffled down a corridor lined with dull-gray tile and institutional-green walls that held no pictures, only rules.

Emily started to tremble as she looked into each scarred cubicle. Young men, old men, men of all sizes and colors peered back at her. She saw his eyes first— hazel, like hers, tears threatening to fall. *Don't you dare cry, Dad*, she thought.

Emily sat. She lifted the phone.

She watched Dad lift the phone.

"Hey." She smiled.

"Hi, Em," he said.

Emily sat silent. *What the heck am I supposed to say now?* She squirmed.

"How are you, Dad?" It sounded so stupid, but she couldn't think of anything else.

"Fine. You?"

She shrugged. "Okay, I guess. I'm working and doing pretty good in school."

Dad raised his eyebrows and ran his fingers through clean, short blond hair. "Can't believe they put you in school. You're almost sixteen and can drop out like I did."

"They let me start as a sophomore. I thought I'd drop out in January, but I kind of like it. I'm thinking I may stay and graduate. Maybe go to college."

"Sounds like a big plan. How are you doing?"

"Not bad. Miki and Da-Shawn are good people."

"Thanks for your letters. Miki sounds like a nice woman. I appreciate her keeping you for me."

Christ, it sounds like I'm an animal in the zoo, Emily thought. "She is a nice woman. And her husband is a nurse. How funny is that?"

Dad smiled. "Men can be nurses." He held up a bandaged hand. "You'll never guess who did this to me."

Emily waited for his answer.

"Remember that guy who gave me my last job? Frank. He's in here for whacking some crazy lady over the head with a shovel. He got mad when I laughed and told him old ladies were all he could handle. Ain't that funny?"

Emily didn't laugh. There was nothing funny about Frank. "Speaking of jobs, guess what, Dad? I got a job for you when you get out."

"A job? Who'd hire a junkie?"

"Father Ron. The custodian that works at St. Jude's—that's his church—is retiring a month after you get out. Father Ron said he'd hire you if you promised to stay clean."

"You can tell your priest friend that I'm clean. I'm in a recovery program here. It's for drunks like me. Got my fourth-month chip last week. Sober sixteen weeks. Can you believe it?"

"Well, you don't have much of a chance to get drunk in jail, do you?"

"Guess not." Dad smiled and then added, "I gotta find me a place to stay when I get out. I was thinkin' about moving into St. Gerard's until I can put some cash away."

"There's a room in the church that you can stay in. No more sleeping in homeless shelters or cars."

"Is there room for you, Em?" Dad asked.

Emily looked down. "No, Dad. I want to stay with Miki until I graduate. Mrs. Allen, the guidance counselor, said I should qualify for a bazillion scholarships. I still want to be a designer."

Dad laughed. "Well, well, well, my Em with big ideas. What about that art show you're having at school. When is it?"

"Next week. I hope I win and sell my sketches. All the money raised goes to St. Gerard's."

"You'll win. I have faith in you."

"Remember, Dad, I told you that I would have a mansion and a swimming pool, and make lots of money with my designs." Emily smiled at the thought; but then, without a warning, the hairs on her arms stood at attention. Looking up, she saw it—the dragon's evil stare as it passed behind her dad. She shivered.

Dad frowned. "You okay, Em?"

Frank stopped and stared. His wrinkled face held a malevolent grin. He pursed his lips and threw her a kiss. Then he waved and continued on his way. She watched her dad turn around as Frank passed.

"He's a bad man, Em."

"I know, Dad. I know." She couldn't begin to tell him about that frightening night last summer. What good would it do? Her dad felt bad enough as it was.

"Hey, I owe you something."

"You don't owe me anything, Dad."

"First thing I want to do when I get out is have a big piece of apple pie with you. I still owe you one, Em."

"Sounds like a plan."

Emily felt a hand on her shoulder. She turned to see the guard standing behind her. "Time's up."

Emily nodded and turned to see tears falling from her dad's eyes. She took a deep breath but couldn't stop the flood of uninvited tears. She put her hand to the window. He put his there too. "Gotta go, Dad. I'll see you soon."

"I love you, Em."

"I love you too, Dad." She hung up the phone and stood, willing herself to leave. She watched her dad hang up the phone as well. Neither of them moved.

"It's time," the guard said.

Emily turned and followed the rest of the visitors out. She sobbed and fell into Miki's arms when she reached the waiting room.

That night, after dinner, Emily closed the door to her room and wrapped herself in a blanket to help ward off a chill that followed her from the visit with Dad. She pulled out her journal. Before writing anything, she drew a picture of her dad's hand holding hers.

> OMG. I saw Dad for the first time since July. Even though he looked good—clean hair for a change—the orange jumpsuit freaked me out.

Talking to him on the phone with a wall of glass between us was awkward. I could see him, but I couldn't hug him. And to top off a terrible experience, that perv, that creep, that monster was there. I can't seem to get rid of him. He is such a sicko. Makes me want to puke when I see him. I'm still shaking.

CHAPTER 24

"I wonder where they are." Eli held Emily's hand as they walked the hallway looking for her sketches. Even though a week had passed, she was still unnerved by the visit with her dad. Eli had questioned her about her whereabouts the day after Thanksgiving. She wasn't ready yet to reveal that part of her life. Not to Eli. Not to anyone. It would stay tucked away, hidden like those proverbial skeletons that inhabit family closets. But Miki and Da-Shawn's warning about lying worried her. What would Eli do if he ever found out?

"Look, there's my sister's attempt at art." Eli pointed to a table filled with vases, bowls, and dishes.

Emily picked up Ava's Asian scallop bowl. "Miki gave her this idea." She looked down to see a Sold sign. "Wow, someone bought it already."

Eli laughed. "Probably my parents."

Emily rolled her eyes. "Give your sister a little more credit. This is good."

As they walked past Mr. Hunt's door, Eli suddenly pulled Emily into the alcove. "What are we doing here?" She looked up into his eyes.

"Just wanted to get you alone for a minute." He put his hand under her chin and tilted her head up.

Emily watched his eyes soften, then close. *He's going to kiss me.* She felt a tingling sensation travel through her body as her face lit up fire-red.

What am I going to do? I totally don't know how to do this.

She closed her eyes as his lips brushed hers. Warm, soft, silky, gentle—like the caress of an unexpected summer breeze.

"Peppermint."

Emily's eyes flew open. "What?"

"Peppermint. You taste like peppermint." Eli kissed her again.

"Busted."

They turned to see Ava standing behind them with her hands on her hips. "I wondered where you two went."

"You're enjoying this, aren't you, little sis?"

"Of course, it's not often I have something on you," Ava said.

Emily envied the teasing between the siblings. She wondered what life would be like if her brother had lived. "You sold your bowl," she said. "How cool is that?"

"My parents probably bought it." Ava laughed.

Eli grabbed Emily's hand and pulled her down the hall. "Let's look for your sketches."

"I know where they are," Ava said. "Follow me."

They passed the SADD bulletin board. Hanging next to the picture of a smiling Joy Jarrell were Emily's four dress designs. An honorable mention certificate was tacked to one of them.

"Whoa! These are amazing, Em. I didn't know you had this kind of talent," Eli said.

"I told you, Eli. I told you that Emily was a real artist." Ava frowned at her brother.

"I wonder if any of these will sell," Emily mused.

"Maybe my parents will buy one. After all, they bought Ava's bowl." Eli nudged Ava, who hit him on the shoulder.

"That dress is beautiful," Ava said as she pointed to one of the drawings. "What made you design it?"

"It was the night I learned about Joy. I knew I'd never go to a high school dance, but I wanted to dream."

"You know, it could be more than a dream," Eli said.

Emily felt the thumping of her heart as Eli touched her arm.

Just then, Emily's phone beeped. She pulled it out of her pocket to see a text from Da-Shawn.

Pick u up in 1/2 hr.

"Da-Shawn's picking me up soon." Emily closed her phone.

"I can drive you home," Eli offered.

"Yeah, right. Da-Shawn won't let me in a car with anyone under thirty-five. You'd think they were my freakin' parents. They're so smothering me." Emily looked up to see Joy staring down at her—unmoving, smiling, never to grow old.

Then there was applause and flashes of light coming from down the hall. "What's going on?" Eli squinted to see what was happening.

"You don't want to go there," Ava said.

"Why not?" Emily started walking toward the commotion.

At the end of the hall, sporting a blue ribbon, hung a dark painting. The background contained splashes of black. A figure of a stooped woman in whites and grays graced one corner.

"It's so depressing," Ava said. "Come on, let's get out of here."

"Why the hurry?"

They turned to see Samantha smiling and posing before the picture.

"Is this yours?" Eli let go of Emily's hand as Sam walked over to the group.

"Of course, Eli. You've already forgotten my talents?" She looked at Emily and continued, "So this is why you dropped me."

"You know the reason, Sam. Emily has nothing to do with it."

"Your painting is amazing." Emily stepped closer to get a better look.

"Yeah, it is. It's even sold for big money. What about yours?"

Emily shook her head. "No one's bought anything yet." Just then, another beep sounded. Emily looked at her phone. "Da-Shawn's outside waiting. Gotta go."

Before she could get away, Eli bent down and kissed her on the cheek. "I'll walk you to the door."

"Oh la la. Looks serious." Samantha turned and sashayed over to a reporter taking pictures for the local paper. "I wonder if Miss Goody-Goody can do for you what I can?"

"What does she mean?" Emily asked Eli as they walked down the hallway.

"Nothing. She's just trying to get to you," Eli said as they reached the door. He held it open for her and waved to Da-Shawn as Emily made her way toward the car.

She slid into the passenger seat and slammed the door a bit harder than she intended.

"Well, I see someone is in a mood. What's up?" Da-Shawn put the car in drive.

"I don't see why I have to be the only one to be picked up. Eli could have driven me home." Emily fastened her seat belt. "After all, I'm almost sixteen, and I will be driving soon."

"You're not sixteen yet." Da-Shawn looked both ways before entering the boulevard.

"Eli's a good driver."

"I'm sure he is, Em. You may be ready for all of this, but I'm not."

"I'm not Joy, Da-Shawn. Just because she was careless doesn't mean I will be." Emily watched him stiffen and regretted the comment. "Sorry, I didn't mean it the way it came out."

Da-Shawn looked straight ahead, saying nothing.

When they arrived home, Emily ran upstairs into her room and threw herself on the bed. She grabbed her journal and opened it to a fresh page.

> Awesome night! Eli kissed me. OMG, I almost fainted when I realized what was going to happen. It felt sooooo good. Soooo sweet. I know it sounds corny, but I was truly weak in the knees. Ava saw us. That was totally embarrassing.

My sketches for the art fair were hanging right by Joy's picture. How weird is that? Da-Shawn and Miki are really getting on my nerves. They won't let me get into a car with Eli. Just because their daughter was killed on a freaking date doesn't mean I will be. It sucks. They are acting like they are my parents. They aren't and I'm not Joy. I do feel awful for something I said to Da-Shawn. It just jumped out of my mouth before I could stop it.

Before closing her journal, she drew a picture of a boy and girl kissing. Then she searched through her purse for some lipstick, applied it, and kissed the page three times.

CHAPTER 25

Emily stood on her tiptoes to hang a golden angel near the top of the Douglas fir that towered in front of a large bay window. Decorated with silver and red ornaments, it was full of lights that twinkled like stars on a moonless night. The scent of pine and bayberry surrounded her, reminding her of the tall pines that grew in the yard of her old house. Memories of past Christmases flooded back, bringing unwanted tears.

Only losers cry, Em.

She shook off melancholy thoughts as she stepped back, tipping her head to see where to place the next ornament.

"The tree looks beautiful. The best one yet. You and Da-Shawn sure know how to pick them." Emily turned to see Miki, standing in the doorway with her arms folded. "I have one more ornament. My sweet angel." Miki reached into the bottom of the box and unwrapped a framed picture of Joy.

Emily pointed to a spot on the tree and said, "Put it here, next to this angel." Sadness washed over her as Miki hung the ornament.

I wish I had a picture of my brother or my mom, she thought.

Miki stood back, admiring the tree, before saying, "You can have a contact visit with your dad on Christmas Day. I found out that it is the only day you can actually be with him instead of talking to him on that nasty phone."

"That'd be good." Emily smiled.

Da-Shawn marched into the room waving an envelope. "Guess what I have here? A card for us from—drum roll, please—none other than our friend Alice."

They sat together on a brown leather sofa. Miki grabbed the envelope from Da-Shawn.

"Hey, woman, I wanted to open it." He tried to grab it back.

Miki grinned as she slid her finger through the top of the envelope, revealing a Christmas card. "I wonder how she's doing. I've written her several times, but this is the first response."

A picture of baby Jesus cradled in his mother's arms graced the front of the card. The words "Blessings to you at this sacred time" greeted them. When Miki opened the card, a picture fell out.

Emily picked it up and laughed. "Look." There was Alice sitting in a rocking chair in front of a blazing fire. She was wrapped in a large colorful blanket, hugging the teddy bear Emily had given her. The tin crown rested on her head. "Do you see it?"

Da-Shawn and Miki looked closer. "Oh my goodness," Miki said. "Alice is smiling. I've never seen her look happy."

"Her medication is working." Da-Shawn took the picture from Emily for a better look.

"She looks, well…almost normal," Emily added.

"She is normal, Em." Da-Shawn handed back the picture. "Why don't you keep this in your room? I know Alice would like you to have it."

Emily nodded.

"Come on, you two, let's light a fire and enjoy the tree."

The three sat on the floor, feeling the warmth emanating from the hearth. Da-Shawn brought out steaming cups of hot chocolate and cookies decorated with green icing for them to nibble on.

Miki reached for Emily's hand. "It's good to have you here. You put the heart back in Christmas for me and Da-Shawn."

Da-Shawn nodded.

"I'm glad I'm here too," Emily said.

Christmas morning found Emily and Da-Shawn scrambling eggs, making coffee, and pouring juice.

"Eww, grits again." Emily wrinkled her nose as she watched Da-Shawn pour the grits into boiling water.

"You're messin' with tradition here, girl." Da-Shawn stirred the mixture. "Christmas morning, we eat our grits with cheese. You'll like it.

"Yeah, yeah, yeah."

"What are you two squabbling about now?" Miki entered the kitchen; she was wearing a thick red robe. She tightened the belt. "Brrr, did you turn up the heat, Da-Shawn?"

"Of course, woman. Want to make sure you're warm enough." He winked at Emily and hugged Miki. "Merry Christmas."

There was a *ding* from Emily's phone. She reddened when Da-Shawn said, "Wonder who could be texting you so early this morning. Could it be...now, let me think...possibly that young man who's captured your fancy. What was his name again?"

Emily playfully punched Da-Shawn on the arm. "You know very well what his name is." She flipped open the phone and read,

Merry Xmas. Did Santa arrive?

Emily smiled and texted back, *How r u?*

Happy. Can't wait to c u.

Me 2.

"Breakfast is served. Let's eat in the living room so we can open presents." Miki picked up her plate and steaming cup of coffee and headed into the living room.

The multicolored lights of the tree cast a warm glow throughout the room. Da-Shawn settled in the large leather recliner beside the fireplace. "Who's going to pass out the gifts?"

"Let me." Emily reached down and picked up a small box wrapped in shiny red paper with a green ribbon. She lifted the bow and said, "To Miki, from DaShawn."

Miki took the package from Emily and looked at Da-Shawn. "Hmm, I wonder what this could be? The Hope Diamond perhaps."

"Shut your trap, woman, and open it," Da-Shawn said.

Miki gently tore off the paper and smiled. "A GPS. How did you ever know this is what I needed?"

"Possibly getting lost going in Atlanta last month."

Miki laughed, kissed Da-Shawn, and said, "Thank you."

"Here's one for you, Da-Shawn, from Miki." Emily handed him a large box wrapped in sparkling red paper topped with a green-and-yellow bow. "Wow, it's heavy."

Da-Shawn ripped the paper off and opened the box to discover a saddle-brown leather coat. Taking it out of the box, he looked at Miki and said, "Woman, you do buy the best things."

"Gotta keep my man warm on these chilly days."

Da-Shawn reached over and pulled Miki closer. Planting a kiss on her cheek, he said, "I can think of better ways to keep me warm."

"Eww, will you two get a room." Emily rolled her eyes and wrinkled up her nose.

Da-Shawn laughed. "Sounds like a good idea." Then he said, "Em, check out the purple box in the back."

Emily reached around the tree and pulled out a large gift with a tag sporting her name. "For me?"

"Of course, for you, girl. Did you think Santa forgot where you lived? Open it," Da-Shawn said.

Emily lifted off the white bow and ran her fingers along one taped edge, careful to save the paper from the first Christmas gift she had received in two years. "A laptop," she gasped.

"We thought you could use a computer of your own," Miki said.

"And it's equipped with a special program for artists. You can do your designs right on the computer," Da-Shawn said.

Emily lifted the shiny black top and ran her fingers over the keys. "This is so totally cool. How can I thank you?"

"Just become the best designer you can be," said Miki. "And we expect the best room in the mansion when we visit."

Emily closed the lid and laughed. "You can come to the mansion anytime. I'll have my chauffeur pick you up in my limo."

"I hope there's a cook too," Da-Shawn said. "I remember your attempt at pizza last week. Woo, wee, burned to a crisp."

Emily rolled her eyes. "Just give me time. I'll match your cooking one of these days. Your grits against my pizza."

"Yeah, yeah. In your face. Let's finish opening presents. You've got to visit your dad this afternoon. What time is Father Ron picking you up?" Da-Shawn reached under the tree and picked up a sparkly green bag.

"Visiting hours are from one to six. He said he would be here at three."

"Are you sure you don't want Da-Shawn and me to go with you?" Miki asked.

"No, you two stay here and keep warm, if you know what I mean." Emily chuckled at her own joke. "I want Dad to meet Father Ron. After all, he is going to give him a job."

CHAPTER 26

The strong smell of bleach assaulted Emily. It made her cringe. Bleach and ammonia—the smell of jail. Clean floors, clean walls, even the women's bathroom was spotless. Emily looked in the mirror one more time after washing her hands. She finger-combed her hair. Wiping her hands on her jeans, she opened the door and walked over to Father Ron.

He smiled. "Are you ready?"

Emily nodded.

"Anderson." They turned to see the husky guard holding their paperwork.

Father Ron and Emily walked over to him, IDs in hand.

The guard looked at each one closely. Pointing to Emily, he said, "You go in that room. Father, you come with me."

Emily stepped into the small room. A bored-looking female guard was leaning on the far wall. "Take off your boots, and hand them to me."

Emily pulled off the brown leather boots she had received for Christmas and handed them to the guard. She watched the guard slip her hand down to the bottom, feeling for contraband, and then turn them upside down and shake them.

"Hold your arms straight out."

Emily stood still as the guard ran her hands up and down her body, encircling her legs.

"Good. Now, I want you to lean forward and lift the bottom of your bra and shake it."

Emily put her hands beneath her shirt. She lifted her bra and shook it.

"You're good to go," the guard said.

I feel like a criminal, she thought as she exited the small room.

When she stepped back into the waiting room, Father Ron was shaking hands with the male guard.

"Follow me," the guard instructed.

They both trailed behind him—through locked doors and down a long hallway with a shiny tiled floor, unadorned green walls, and the smell of bleach. Emily wrinkled her noise.

The guard unlocked the door to the visiting room. The sound of voices, all talking at once, assaulted Emily like the force of an out-of-control rock concert. People of all ages and colors sat in uncomfortable folding chairs at long tables. Young children looked at tattered books as parents conversed. A woman huddled in one corner with a tattooed young man.

The guard reminded them, "One hug and then you are not allowed to touch the inmate again until you leave. Then one more hug."

"But it's not an inmate—it's my dad. Can I hold his hand?"

"Sorry, miss. Rules are rules." The guard turned and walked away.

Emily spotted Dad as he came through a barred door. Tears filled her eyes. She heard his mantra in her head: *Only losers cry.* He waved and pointed to a table in the corner.

Emily and Father Ron made their way through the Christmas crowd. Emily hugged her dad for the first time in months. It felt warm and comforting. "Dad, I want you to meet my friend Father Ron."

"Carl Anderson." Dad shook Father Ron's hand. "Em's told me a lot about you. How you helped her in the beginning and about the job offer. Why don't we sit here?"

"I've heard a lot about you too." Father Ron pulled out a metal chair and sat at the pockmarked table.

"Dad, look at my boots. Totally cool. Miki and Da-Shawn gave them to me for Christmas."

"I wish I had something to give you, Em." Dad looked down before placing his elbows on the table.

"Next year, Dad. Next year, we'll be together. And not here."

Emily felt someone bump into her chair. She scooted closer to the table to let people through, but then, she heard, "Well, well, well, little girl. Fancy meetin' you here." Her heart began to race, and her hands shook. She turned to see Frank looming over her.

"Hey, Frank, watch where you're goin'," Dad said. "Can't believe you're still here. Thought they were going to take you away before Christmas."

Frank snorted. "Got my lawyer to get me an appeal. That crazy woman came at me first. I was just defendin' myself. Ain't that right, little girl?"

Emily watched her father frown. "What are you talkin' about?"

"Why, your little girl was there when it happened. Maybe I can make her my star witness. What do you think?" Frank touched Emily on the shoulder.

She jumped as if an electric current was surging through her. She pushed away his hand. "Get away from me, you freak."

"Now, is that the way to talk to an old friend?"

"Is there trouble here?" A guard with his hands folded over a beer belly stood close to them.

"No, Officer. No trouble. Just sayin' hi to an old friend here." Frank winked at Emily and walked over to another table. She watched him sit by an elderly lady.

"You were there when Frank assaulted that woman?" Dad asked.

Emily nodded. "He'd been doing odd jobs for Miki. He was at the store that day. He can't make me testify, can he?"

"He's bluffin', Em. Everyone in here is innocent. Just ask them. He's goin' away soon."

Emily listened while Father Ron and Dad talked about the job and living arrangements that would be available after his release. She looked over her shoulder to see Frank peering at her. She turned her back to him, but she could still feel his eyes piercing her flesh like a knife ripping into her innocence.

When it was time to leave, Emily hugged her dad and watched him walk through the barred door. Frank shuffled behind Dad, turned, and blew Emily a kiss. Goose bumps tiptoed up her arms as a shudder ran through her.

"Is there anything you want to tell me about that man, Emily?" Father Ron asked as they walked down the long hallway back to the waiting room.

Emily shook her head. "I'm good."

"You sure?"

"I'm sure." *This* secret would be forever hidden.

CHAPTER 27

"I still don't understand why you couldn't come to dinner." Eli frowned as he held Emily's hand.

"Miki and I helped Father Ron clean up from all the festivities after today's Mass." Emily ran her fingers through her hair, trying to figure out a way to change the conversation.

"I could have helped too. Why didn't you ask me?"

Why don't you just freakin' let it go, she thought and then said aloud, "You were with your family, Eli. That's more important at Christmas."

"You are important to me, Em," Eli said, leaning over to kiss her.

Their conversation was interrupted when Miki entered the living room, carrying a tray holding two steaming mugs and a plate of frosted sugar cookies. "Okay, you two. Hot cider and cookies. The perfect way to end Christmas Day. So, did Santa bring you anything, Eli?" she asked.

"Some clothes and a new impossible-to-lose watch," Eli said and held up his arm to show off the new watch. "How about you, Mrs. Jarrell?"

"Mr. Jarrell thinks I can't find my way out of a box, so he gave me a GPS for my car." She put the cider and cookies on the coffee table. "I'd join you, but I have a feeling that you two would rather be alone."

Emily picked up one of the mugs, wrapping her hands around it for warmth and inhaling the cinnamon aroma. She took a sip. "Hmm. This tastes spicy."

"Not as spicy as you." Eli kissed her again before handing her a box wrapped in shiny red paper and a large gold bow. "Merry Christmas. I hope you like it."

Emily smiled as she unwrapped the gift. "It's beautiful." She lifted out a safari-green cardigan and held it up to her. "How does it look?" she asked.

"Beautiful. Just like you. It makes your eyes look green."

Emily looked down. She unfastened the jeweled buttons and slipped it on. "I love it." She walked around to the back of the tree and retrieved a small box. "Here. I have something for you."

Eli took the box. "Hey, don't I get a kiss."

Emily laughed and gave him a quick peck on the cheek.

She watched him remove the wrapping and lift the lid off the box. "Sweet." He took out a leather bracelet and fingered the silver emblem that read "Abercrombie and Fitch."

Emily watched him fumble with the clasp. "Here, let me help you put it on."

"It's awesome, Em. Thanks. I have one more thing for you." Eli pulled a small box out of his pocket and handed it to Emily.

"What is it?" she asked.

"Why don't you open it and find out?"

Emily untied the white ribbon that was tied around the light-blue box. "It's from Tiffany's." She looked at Eli before removing the lid. Her eyes widened as she stared at the silver heart pendant nestled on a bed of cotton. "I've never had anything this…this…beautiful."

He smiled. "Let me put it on you."

Emily handed the box back to Eli. "It's too expensive."

Eli shook his head. He took the necklace out of the box and said, "Turn around."

Emily hesitated and then turned. Eli fastened it, placed his hands on her shoulders, and kissed the back of her neck. Emily shivered as she turned around to face him.

They heard a whistle from the entry, and both jumped as they heard Da-Shawn say, "What is that shiny thing hanging around your neck?"

"A gift from Eli," Emily said.

"It's beautiful," Miki said as she playfully swatted at Da-Shawn. "Beats a GPS."

"Hey now, woman, I was going to get you a new vacuum cleaner. Where's your appreciation?" Then he added, "Come on, we need to leave these kids alone. Think you can find your way upstairs, or do you need the GPS?"

Miki gave Da-Shawn a loving push. "Funny."

As soon as the Jarrells were out of sight, Eli drew Emily closer. "I'm glad we're alone." He kissed her with more passion and let his hand slip up her blouse, reaching toward her breast.

"What the heck are you doing?" Emily grabbed his hand.

"It's time, Em."

"Time for what?" Emily frowned.

"You know, for us to get closer."

"Exactly what do you mean by *closer*?" She scooted away from Eli.

"Come on, Em. Do I have to spell it out for you? We've been seeing each other for a while."

"Only a month, Eli."

"Yeah. Most people do it on the first date," he said.

"Well, I'm not one of those people. And besides, Miki and Da-Shawn are here," she said. "What if they hear us or come downstairs?"

"They won't hear a thing. I'm real good."

"I don't want to take a chance. And besides, I'm not ready for anything that…that…serious. Not yet."

"Then when? How long am I supposed to wait?" he asked.

Emily looked away, gathering her thoughts.

Both sat in silence. *Great, now what am I supposed to do?* she wondered.

Eli suddenly stood up and reached for his coat. "Time for me to go."

"Don't go yet," Emily said. "Let's talk."

"I'm done talking. Call me if you change your mind about—"

"Come on, Eli. Don't be mad." Emily stood and tried to kiss him.

He ignored the gesture. "I'm not mad, Em. Just disappointed. I thought we had something here."

"We do. But you're asking for too much."

Eli walked to the front door, turned, and said, "I'll call you."

Emily watched as he backed out of the driveway until the taillights of his car disappeared in the darkness.

She turned out the lights of the Christmas tree and tiptoed upstairs. Miki stepped out of the bathroom and said, "Has Eli already left?"

"Yes, he had to get home to do a family thing." Emily swallowed the lie along with the lump stuck in her throat.

"Did you have a nice Christmas?" Miki asked.

"The best. Thanks for everything." Emily hugged Miki and headed down the hall. She opened the door to her room and turned to see Miki watching her.

"Are you sure everything is okay?" Miki asked.

Emily nodded, fighting tears. She closed the door and flopped on her bed. She buried her head in her pillow and sobbed. *I can't do this, not yet. But I can't lose Eli.*

She pulled out her journal, picked up a pen, and sat staring at a blank page.

> My first Christmas—in so long—like the ones I used to have with Mom, Dad, and Danny. The day started off great. Miki and Da-Shawn gave me the coolest gifts. It was fun being a part of a real family.
>
> Then it got a little weird. First I went to see Dad. I got to give him a hug and talk to him without using that dirty, nasty, germy phone.

But I must be cursed. Everywhere I go that perv shows up. Today he was in the jail visiting room. I thought he went to prison. He got so close I could smell his foul, evil body. Ewww. I wanted to hurl when he touched me.

Next, Eli came over. I had to lie to him about where I went. He must never know about the before me, or Dad, or jail—never. He gave me a beautiful necklace.

Emily opened the blue box and picked up the necklace. She held the heart next to her cheek before placing it back on its cotton bed.

But he started pushing me to do the deed. I think I'm in love with him, but I sure am not ready to do *it*. This boyfriend/girlfriend thing is getting too complicated.

She picked up the pencil again and drew a picture of Eli kissing her and the necklace resting on her chest.

CHAPTER 28

The next day, Emily awoke to the sound of her cell phone. She sat up, stretched, and grabbed the phone off the nightstand.

Eli!

She was disappointed to see Ava's photo on her screen. She took a settling breath before she answered.

"Hi, Ava."

"Did I wake you?"

"Yeah, but it's time. What's up?"

"What's up with you and Eli? He came home early last night. And I heard him talking to Sam this morning."

Emily threw off the covers and reached for her robe. "Sam? Why?"

"I don't know. I think he wants to see her today," Ava whispered into the phone.

"We had kind of a fight last night, but he said he'd call me. Why would he want to see Sam?" Emily asked.

"Only one reason I can think of," Ava said.

Emily finger-combed her hair as she listened to Ava. "What do you mean? What reason?"

"Come on, Em. You're not that innocent, are you? Eli and Sam were hot and heavy before he started seeing you."

Emily sat back against her pillow. "You mean they…" She couldn't bring herself to finish.

"Yeah, every chance they could," Ava said.

"I know Eli tells you a lot, but he actually told you something like that? I can't believe it," Emily responded.

"No, Sam bragged about it all over school."

"Great. What am I going to do?" Emily asked.

"Have you two, you know, done it?"

"No! I don't do stuff like that." Emily's voice quivered at the thought.

"You mean you've never hooked up with anyone?" Ava asked.

"Never," Emily said.

"Does Eli know that you're a virgin?"

"No way. That stuff is private. Nobody's business."

"Well, if you want to hang on to my brother, you better think about it."

"What if I'm not ready for a commitment like that?" Emily asked.

"That's your decision. But guys today expect it," Ava said.

"Have you?" Emily knew that Ava was not dating anyone at the moment.

"Not yet. To tell you the truth, I find boys a bit… how can I say it…gross." Changing the subject, Ava said, "Let's get together this afternoon. I have to make some exchanges. We can meet in the mall."

"Sounds like a plan. But I have to ask Da-Shawn for a ride." Emily sighed.

"Around two o'clock?"

"Okay."

"I'll let you know if I hear any more Sam news. Bye." Ava hung up.

Emily snapped her cell phone shut and reached for the box that contained the silver heart. *What am I going to do now?*

Sitting back on the bed, she retrieved her journal from the nightstand and reread last night's entry. She picked up a pencil.

> Hooking up. Now that's an interesting way to say it. I want to go out with, be with, date Eli, but hooking up? I'm not sure I'm ready for something so personal. I wonder what it is like being naked with a boy. Or having him touch me in—those places.

Emily put down the journal, stood up, and wrapped herself in a silk robe. She tied it at the waist and slipped into her fluffy pink slippers. Walking to the window, she looked down to see a blanket of fresh snow covering the trees and bushes. Icicles, like jagged spikes, hung from the eaves. She paced and thought before picking up the journal and continuing.

> I'll be sixteen next month. Maybe it's time. But what if Eli and Sam get back together? Do I call him? I can't discuss this with Ava. And if Miki and Da-Shawn knew, they would go ballistic. Father Ron? Definitely not.

She turned to the picture she had drawn the previous night: Eli kissing her. Biting the end of the pencil, she drew an enormous heart around it and nodded her head. The decision was made.

"I'll text you when I'm ready to come home. Thanks for the ride, Da-Shawn." Emily closed the car door and headed toward the mall.

Ava was waiting for her in front of Aeropostale as planned. "I have to return this pair of jeans, and then we can walk around and see who's here."

Emily smiled and said, "Okay by me. Why are you returning the jeans?"

"Too small. My parents still think I'm a preteen, I guess. They treat me like a baby." Ava walked into the store and stood by the register.

"I'm almost sixteen, and Da-Shawn won't let me get in a car with anyone. How lame is that?"

"Pretty lame," Ava said. "And overprotective."

After Ava returned the jeans, the pair decided to walk toward the food court. As they entered, Emily suddenly stopped and pulled Ava in front of her. "We can't go there."

Ava peered into the crowd and spotted Eli with Samantha. "I knew it. He's with her."

"Let's get out of here," Emily said.

"No, you go. I'm going to do some spying on big bro. I'll meet you in fifteen minutes at Hot Tees."

Emily ducked behind a kiosk and left. She turned around to see an innocent-looking Ava walking toward Eli.

Hot Tees was full of people returning unwanted Christmas gifts. Flipping through black T-shirts, Emily pulled one out, pretending to be interested, all the while looking at the door, anxious for Ava to enter. An employee standing nearby winked at her and said, "That's a good choice."

Oh great. Emily felt the blood rush to her face, and she almost dropped the shirt when she zeroed in on the words written in large white letter on the front: I Just Had Sex.

Awkward! This is so totally embarrassing, she thought as she hung the shirt back on the rack and moved to the jewelry section. *Ava, where are you?*

The beeping of her phone interrupted her thoughts. It was a text from Ava.

On my way.

"What did you find out?" Emily asked when her friend arrived.

"Plenty. Sam was furious with Eli. Told him that she wasn't his whore and to quit calling her."

"So, they aren't going to hook up?" Emily asked.

"Doesn't look like it," Ava said and pulled out the same T-shirt that Emily had almost dropped. "Hey, you should get this."

"Funny. Let's get out of here," Emily said.

That night, Emily reread her last two journal entries. She picked up her cell phone and flipped it open. Then shut. Then open. Then shut. She placed it back on the nightstand and ran her fingers through her hair before picking it up again. She flipped it open and stared at the blank screen. Pushing the Message icon, she typed "Call me," scrolled down to Eli's name, and hit Send.

Flipping to a fresh page in her journal, she wrote in her neat feminine handwriting,

I think I'm ready.

CHAPTER 29

"The roads are getting slippery, Em. Maybe you and Eli should wait. You can always go to the movies tomorrow," Miki said.

"The theater is not far. And besides, Da-Shawn has a jeep," Emily pleaded.

"She's right, Miki. It'll be okay. And the movie ends at what time?" Da-Shawn turned to Emily.

"Eleven thirty," Emily lied. "Eli can bring me home. You don't have to wait up. Everything will be okay. I promise."

"You know the rule, Em. I don't want you in a car with a teen driver. Not yet. And definitely not tonight when there's ice on the roads."

The phone rang.

"I wonder who that could be." Miki picked up the receiver and looked at the screen. "It's Alice." She pushed the Talk button. "Alice, how are you?"

"I must talk to Emily. It's important," Alice whispered.

Miki frowned and handed the phone to Emily. "She wants to talk to you."

Emily reached for the receiver and said, "Hi, Alice. What's up?"

"Be careful. Very careful."

Emily frowned. "How are you?"

"I'm fine. But you need to be careful. Very careful."

"Are you trying to scare me?"

"No, but danger is close."

"But the bad man is gone, Alice. He's in jail."

"Be wary." The phone went dead.

Emily stood there for a minute, holding the silent receiver before looking at Miki and Da-Shawn. "That was weird."

"How is Alice doing?" Miki asked.

"I don't know. She gave me one of her famous warnings. They always creep me out." Emily handed the phone to Miki.

"Let me call her back and find out what she meant." Miki punched in Alice's number, only to hear a busy signal. "I'll try her later. By the way, you look beautiful. Eli's a lucky guy."

You don't know how lucky. Aloud, she said, "Thanks."

"Come on, Em. Time's a-wastin'." Da-Shawn opened the front door.

Emily texted Eli as they neared the theater.

He stood outside, his coat flapping in the wind despite the cold. He opened the car door for Emily when Da-Shawn pulled up to the curb. He said, "Thanks for bringing Emily, Mr. Jarrell." He took her hand as she exited the car. "Be careful. It's slippery here."

"I'll be back at eleven thirty. Have fun," Da-Shawn said.

They waved good-bye and pretended to head toward the theater.

"I've been looking forward to this night for weeks," Eli said as he and Emily watched Da-Shawn pull away from the curb. "Does Da-Shawn suspect anything?"

Emily smiled. "No. I'm fairly good at keeping secrets."

They watched until he turned onto the street and his taillights faded into the night.

Eli grabbed Emily's hand. "Come on."

Once they were in the car, Emily buckled her seat belt. Eli started the engine and cranked up the heat. "It won't take long for the car to warm up."

As he started to pull out of the parking space, Emily asked, "Aren't you going to fasten your seatbelt?"

"I'm good, Em," Eli replied and pulled into traffic.

"Where are we going?" Emily asked.

"I know a great place outside of town. It's secluded. No one will bother us," Eli said.

The drive took thirty minutes. Eli turned off the main highway and onto a small country lane. He eventually stopped underneath a grove of trees. He switched off the lights and then the engine. The full moon illuminated the inside of the car. Emily unbuckled her seatbelt and scooted next to Eli. He pulled her close and kissed her. Gently at first, and then she felt his tongue slip between her lips. She shivered with desire as his hand touched her breast.

"I think the backseat would be more comfortable," he said.

A flashback to another time, in the backseat of a rusted Toyota, blindsided Emily. She started to shake.

"Are you having second thoughts?" Eli asked.

"No, just a little cold," she said.

"You won't be in a minute." Emily watched as Eli took off his coat, slipped out of his sweater, and removed his shirt. "Your turn."

She unzipped her jacket. He reached for the buttons of her sweater. "No, I'll do it," Emily said.

Eli watched her take off her sweater and then kissed her again. She felt his urgency as he fumbled with the buttons on her blouse. Her breathing became rapid as his hand traveled down and touched the swell of her breast. Again, she started to shake.

Eli looked up and said, "Let me get the blanket in the back." He turned and reached over the seat. That was when Emily saw it. The head of a dragon tattooed on his left shoulder.

Fear and panic washed over her like the fury of a tsunami destroying everything in its path. She frantically started to button her blouse.

"What are you doing, Em?" Eli held up the blanket. "This will keep us warm."

Emily grabbed her sweater and said, "I can't do this."

"Sure you can." Eli placed the blanket around her shoulders and started to kiss her neck.

"No, no, no. I want to go home," Emily said as her heart pounded, racing at the speed of a rocket during liftoff.

"You've got to be kidding. Relax, it's going to be okay." Eli unzipped his pants.

Suddenly, the vision of another man unzipping his pants slammed into Emily with tornado force. She screamed.

"Calm down. It'll be okay." Eli frowned.

Emily sat there, shaking so hard her teeth chattered. She watched Eli grab his shirt. "Okay, okay, settle down. I'll take you home." He pulled his sweater over his head and added, "What's wrong with you?"

"I...I...I just can't do this. I'm sorry."

"'Sorry doesn't cut it, Em. You led me on. You promised." He started the engine and put the car in reverse. "I didn't know you were such a loser."

Emily started to cry as he pulled out onto the highway.

Eli slammed his foot on the accelerator. The car hit a patch of ice and began to fishtail. Headlights from an oncoming car blinded him.

"Oh crap," was the first sound that reached her before her world began to spin out of control. She closed her eyes and grabbed the strap of her seatbelt.

Eli twisted the steering wheel to avoid the approaching car. The spinning stopped.

Emily felt jarring bumps as the car plunged down the ravine. Lights bounced up and down from treetop to ground. Tree. Ground. Tree. Ground. Suddenly, the car flipped, slipping on its top; and then with a resounding crash, it slammed into an enormous tree. Emily's head slammed against the passenger window. Everything went black.

CHAPTER 30

The next sound Emily heard was the repetitive beeping of monitors. She opened her eyes and stared at the bright lights in the ceiling. Wiggling to find some relief from the uncomfortable gurney, she let her eyes focus on a nurse adjusting a bag hanging from a pole next to her.

"You're awake." The nurse smiled. "That's good. Can you tell me how you are feeling?"

Emily groaned. "I hurt all over."

The nurse nodded. "I'm not surprised. Let me get the doctor."

As the nurse rushed out of the small cubicle, Emily heard the doors to the emergency room burst open. "Where is she?" It was Da-Shawn's voice, deep and insistent.

"Room 19, Da-Shawn. She just woke up."

The curtain flew open, and Da-Shawn entered like a wild man running from a hungry bear. His face drained of color. He looked at Emily before blurting out, "What in the world were you thinking?"

Miki stepped in and put a hand on his shoulder. "Calm down, Da-Shawn." She walked over to Emily and took her hand. "Are you okay?"

"Not sure." Emily looked into Miki's ashen face. "My arm hurts."

"That's because it's broken in two places." The doctor stepped into the cubicle holding an x-ray. He shook Da-Shawn's hand and kissed Miki on the cheek. "And you've got a nasty concussion. You're going to be okay, but we're going to keep you here for a couple days. Thank goodness she was wearing a seatbelt. The boy wasn't so lucky."

Emily froze. "Eli! Tell me. Is he—"

The doctor turned to her. "He's in surgery." Then he said to Da-Shawn, "Internal bleeding. His dad's in there to observe. We'll know in a couple hours how bad it is."

"It's all my fault," Emily said, her voice cracking. "It's all my fault."

Miki looked down and shook her head. "It was an accident, Em. It wasn't anyone's fault. The streets were slippery."

An orderly pushed the curtain aside and said, "We need to get the patient to orthopedics and get that arm casted."

"I'm going with you." Da-Shawn followed the orderly as he pushed the gurney out of the cubicle.

"I'll go and sit with Annie and Ava, see if I can find out any more information on Eli's condition," Miki said.

Emily peered at the anchor tattoo on Da-Shawn's forearm as he guided the gurney through the bright hallways of the hospital. When they reached the orthopedic wing, the orderly swiped his badge through the slot of a small box that stood guard next to the doors. With a *whoosh*, the large doors magically opened. Wooziness took hold of her as she was wheeled into a large room bright with lights. A masked doctor leaned over her and said, "Relax. Everything will be okay." Then she fell asleep.

The clinking of chains woke Emily. She looked up to see Dad standing by her bed, his hands and feet in shackles. A uniformed guard stood behind him.

With unfocused eyes and a voice that sounded as though her mouth was full of cotton, she said, "What are you doing here?"

"Father Ron and the jail chaplain are pals. They managed to pull some strings and get permission so I could come see you, Em. You scared the livin' daylights out of me. I thought...I thought..."

Emily smiled in spite of the pain. "Is there anybody that man doesn't know? I'm good, Dad. Well, kind of." Emily tried to focus on the clock that hung on the wall opposite the bed. "What time is it?"

Father Ron stepped close to the bed. "It's eight in the morning."

"Eli?" Emily tried to sit up, but the weight of the cast and the pain from the concussion kept her still.

"Eli's out of surgery," Father Ron said. "He's going to be okay, but he has a long road to recovery. His side of the car rammed into the tree, causing broken ribs that punctured one lung and lacerated his liver. Do you know why he wasn't wearing a seatbelt?"

She thought about saying, *He was in a hurry to get away from me.* But instead, she said, "I don't know."

Everyone turned their heads at the sound of a soft knock on the door. The guard walked over and opened it. Emily could hear Ava's voice. "I want to come in and see Emily."

"Sorry, miss, but you have to wait until the prisoner departs," said the guard. He looked at his watch. "We should be leaving in fifteen minutes." He closed the door and resumed his stance behind Dad.

What am I going to do? Emily thought. *Ava's going to find out.*

"Is that a friend of yours?" asked Dad.

"Yes. It's Eli's sister," Emily said.

Dad nodded. "I see. Hopefully, she will be able to tell you more about your boyfriend."

The guard looked at his watch again and said, "Ten more minutes, Anderson."

As Emily was about to speak, the doctor came in. "How's the patient today?"

The grogginess was beginning to wear off. But Emily's head felt like a baseball bat had played nine innings with her skull. "I'm good. But my head still hurts."

"Give it time. You'll feel better."

"When can I go home?" Emily asked.

"Your signs are all good, but I want you to enjoy our hospitality a few more days," he responded.

"Eli. How's Eli?" she asked.

"Don't worry about your friend," the doctor said. "You need to rest and concentrate on your healing right now. I'll be back later to check on you."

After he left, the guard said, "It's time, Anderson."

Dad bent down and kissed Emily on the forehead. "Bye, honey. I'll see you soon." He squeezed her hand and then turned and shuffled toward the door.

"Bye, Dad. I love you," she said.

He looked back at her. "I love you too."

As Dad exited the room, Emily heard the guard say, "You can go in now."

Ava entered the room. "Who was that guy?"

"It's a long story," Emily said. "How's Eli?"

"He's going to be okay, Em. Don't worry. The surgery went well. But you, look at you. What happened?"

"Another long story. Can I see Eli?"

"Not yet." Da-Shawn entered the room carrying a tray. "First, breakfast. The specialty of the house. My house, that is." With a flourish, he lifted the silver lid that hid her meal. "Tada! Grits, made this morning with my very own special guaranteed-to-make-you-well ingredients."

Emily looked at the plate filled with scrambled eggs, grits, and rye toast. "I'm not very hungry."

Da-Shawn set it on the table beside her bed while Miki handed her a glass of freshly squeezed orange juice. "You need to eat," she said.

"I need to see Eli first." Emily took a sip of the juice.

"I need to get back to ICU," Ava said. "I think he can have visitors when he gets into a regular room. I'll be back later and fill you in."

"Thanks, Ava. Tell Eli…tell him…I'm sorry."

Ava nodded and hurried out the door.

Doctors and nurses rushed in and out of Emily's room the entire morning. Ava didn't return. Emily picked up the phone to find out what was happening when Miki entered the room. "How are you feeling?"

"I wish everyone would quit asking me that. I feel like crap." Emily struggled to sit up.

"Here, let me help you." Miki adjusted the pillow and pushed a button to raise the bed and then propped up Emily's still-aching head. "How's that?"

"Better. Can I see Eli now?"

Miki sat in a flower-covered recliner and looked out the window as she tried to find the words. Finally, she said, "Dr. Dawson ran into your dad in the elevator."

"That's all I need. What happened? He didn't find out, did he?"

Miki nodded. "Secret's out, Em. Your dad was talking about you to the guard. Dr. Dawson put two and two together. And—"

"And what?" Emily winced as she turned her head to look at Miki.

"And he came to me and asked me to fill him in. So, I told him the whole story."

"You could have lied, you know. What did he say?"

"He didn't take it well. He was angry and felt we all deceived him. He doesn't want you to see Eli and asked Ava to stay away from you. I'm sorry, Em. I really am."

"I have to see them. Make them understand why I…why I lied."

"Not yet. Give it some time. Now, the thing for you to do is get some rest." Miki rose and kissed her on the forehead. "I'll be back in a couple of hours."

Crap! Why did you have to show up here, Dad? It's all your fault. She reached for the phone and dialed the operator. "Can you give me the number of Eli Dawson's room?"

"I'm sorry, I'm not allowed to give out that information," the operator replied.

Emily slammed down the phone.

When Miki returned, she had Emily's journal in hand. "I thought you could use this."

"Where did you find it?" Emily asked.

"On your nightstand. I know you like to write in it," Miki said.

"Did you read it?"

"Of course not. I respect your privacy." Miki handed it to Emily.

"Thanks."

That night, after everyone had left, Emily sat up in bed and ran her hand over the cover of her diary. She opened it and read the last entry. With a click of a pen and a fresh page staring at her, she began to write,

> Life sucks. Really, really sucks. Eli and I were about to hook up when I went ballistic. I thought I could do it, but I'm so confused. Do I listen to my heart or my conscience?

She tore the page out, wadded it up, and started again.

Mom once told me that when I had to make a decision, especially a big one, I should first listen to my gut. I ignored that feeling yesterday. My gut was screaming no in so many ways I'm surprised that the world didn't hear it. But I didn't listen. Didn't want to listen.

The second thing Mom said about decision making is to write down all the pros and cons of a situation. So let me start...

Pros:

1. If I hook up with Eli, he will love me more. (I think.)

Cons:

1. It doesn't feel right to me.

2. There are big risks, a.k.a. pregnancy or STDs. (Yeah, yeah, I know, I sound like a freakin' sex education teacher).

3. I just don't want to do it! Not yet.

Emily closed her journal and set it down on the table beside her bed and then reached for the button that controlled the lights. Before turning off the overhead light, she stared out the window and watched a cloud pass in front of a full moon.

She whispered the only prayer she could remember: "Now I lay me down to sleep..."

CHAPTER 31

It has been said—somewhere—that pain is real but suffering is optional. A broken arm heals, but what about a broken heart? Neither a bandage nor a cast, not even Miki and Da-Shawn's kindness, could fix it. Loneliness, her constant companion, followed Emily into the new year, and she dreaded going back to school.

What would she say to Ava? How could she face Eli? She couldn't avoid them. It was a big school, but not big enough.

"Hi. How's the arm?" Emily looked over to see Ava standing in the middle of the hall.

"It's good. How's Eli?" Emily asked.

"He's got a homebound teacher for now. The doctor said he should be ready to come back to school in about three more weeks."

Emily nodded.

"Em, I'm so sorry I didn't call you. My mom and dad don't want Eli and me to hang with you anymore."

"I know. Maybe if I talk to them...apologize..." Emily reached into her locker to retrieve her dreaded algebra book.

Ava shrugged. "They sort of hold you responsible for the accident. I know it wasn't your fault, but they needed someone to blame. Then there's the story about your dad."

Emily hung her head before asking, "And Eli? Is he still mad?"

"He hasn't said a word about that night. Or you. He stays in his room and plays video games most of the day. He can't play basketball this year. My dad's afraid it'll affect his chances for a scholarship."

"He probably hates me, but I had to keep my dad, you know, a secret. I knew this would happen if anyone found out." Emily closed her locker door.

"I know," Ava said. "Sorry, Em. Hey, your birthday is this weekend. Are you having a party? After all, you know what they say about sweet sixteen."

Wow. Sixteen and my birthday party consists of a priest, a social worker, and my pretend parents. How lame does it get? All I need is Alice to complete the crazy day.

"Happy birthday, dear Emily. Happy birthday to you."

After singing, everyone clapped their hands and urged her to make a wish before blowing out the candles on her cake.

Emily closed her eyes and thought about the tragedy of the past year. She thought of her dad and her mom and Danny. She thought of Eli and Ava, and Miki and Da-Shawn. Because of them, she had a home, security, and even love. All she really wanted, wished for now, was Eli's forgiveness. She opened her eyes, took a breath, and blew out the candles.

Are you going to tell us what you wished for?" Da-Shawn asked.

"Right. You know it won't come true if I tell." Emily poked Da-Shawn in the side.

"It's time to open presents." Miki handed Emily a large blue bag out of which poked green-and-orange tissue paper. "This is from me and Da-Shawn."

She pulled out the tissue to reveal an iPad. "This is awesome. Thank you."

"You're welcome. You kids and your technology. I wish I had all these tools when I was your age," Da-Shawn said.

Josephina gave her a new journal. The black leather cover sported the words, "In the midst of our lives, we must find the magic that makes our souls soar."

Emily embraced Josephina and said, "It's beautiful. Thank you."

"Lots of room for your designs. I'll be able to say I knew you when." Josephina smiled.

Father Ron handed her an envelope with stickers of cars adorning it. She slid her finger along the top and pulled out a card with a large number *16* in front. When she opened it, a certificate fell out. It read, "Sixteen driving lessons. Guaranteed to help you pass your driver's test the first time."

"You're a brave one, Ron," Josephina said.

"Anyone want to help me with this dangerous endeavor?"

"Not I," said Da-Shawn. He sat back in his chair and folded his arms.

"Not I," said Miki as she prepared to cut the cake.

"Not I," said Josephina.

"What a bunch of cowards. I feel like I'm in the middle of a *Chicken Little* story," Emily said.

"I think you mean *Little Red Hen*," Father Ron said.

"Whatever." Emily rolled her eyes. Just as she was about to reach for a piece of cake, the phone rang. She answered it and heard the usual spiel, "You have a call from a correctional institute….if you accept the call, please press one."

She grinned, pressed one, and said, "Hi Dad."

"Happy birthday, Em," he said. "Are you having a big sweet-sixteen party?"

"A party, but not big," she said.

"I have a present for you. Well, sort of. My attorney visited me yesterday. I may be able to get out sooner than I thought. All I have to do is complete the Freedom in Recovery program. It will end in March. I'm already scheduled to go to a halfway house until the job with the church opens up. What do you think?"

"Now, that's a great gift, Dad," Emily said. "By then, I should have my driver's license. I can pick you up."

"Now, there's a scary thought." Dad laughed. "But to tell you the truth, I look forward to it. Can't believe my little girl is growing up so fast."

"Get used to it, Dad."

"I guess I don't have a choice. How are you feeling? The arm healing?"

"Yeah, I should get my cast off soon."

"Are you coming to visit tomorrow?"

"Of course."

"Oh, by the way, Em, you don't have to worry about seeing Frank. The guards took him away New Year's Eve. I heard they sent him up to Arrowhead. It's got a rep for being a bad prison."

Emily smiled and thought, *Maybe this will be a better year. Good riddance to that piece of trash.*

Before he hung up Dad said, "I look forward to your visits. See you tomorrow, Em. Happy birthday. I love you."

"I love you too, Dad. Bye." She hung up.

"I'm glad your dad was able to call." Miki handed Da-Shawn a huge piece of cake.

"Yeah. He said he may get out in March. That's so soon." Emily turned to look at Father Ron.

"His job is secure, Em," Father Ron said. "But, you know, he can't start until July.

Emily shook her head. "He said that he has been accepted into a halfway house."

Josephina said, "That's good, Emily. It'll be a safe place for him. It's hard for some addicts to stay clean when they get out of jail. Did he say which one?"

"No, but I think Dad is ready to change. He has to. He's my only family."

Da-Shawn stood and hugged Emily. "Not your only family, Em. You have all of us."

CHAPTER 32

"Am I in trouble?" Emily parked herself in the lime-green chair and looked up at the guidance secretary.

"I don't think so, dear. Mrs. Allen has something she wants to discuss with you."

Emily watched another student leave her guidance counselor's office and shut the door. The clock ticked one—she was going to miss algebra.

The door opened. Mrs. Allen smiled at her. "Won't you come in, Emily."

Wiping her hands on her jeans, Emily rose and walked into the room. She sat on the now-familiar overstuffed sofa and inhaled the lavender fragrance that emitted from one of those lame plug-ins. It was supposed to make people relax, but Emily couldn't stop wiggling her foot as she waited for Mrs. Allen to speak.

Mrs. Allen sat at her paper-strewn desk.

"Am I in trouble?" Emily asked.

"No." Mrs. Allen looked up and smiled at her. "I have something I want to discuss with you. We're waiting for another student. But first, how are you feeling?"

"I'm good. My arm comes out of the cast next week. Just in time for my driving lessons." Emily laughed and continued, "Da-Shawn keeps teasing me about doing the dishes. Says I owe him six weeks for all he's done."

There was a soft tap at the door. "Come in," Mrs. Allen said.

Sam entered and asked, "What's up? I'm missing a science test."

"Emily, you know Samantha White, don't you?"

Emily nodded as Sam sat down next to her. She was surprised to see Samantha conservatively dressed in skinny gray jeans and a ruffled pink turtleneck topped with a teal cardigan sweater. It was such a change from the miniskirts and low-cut tops she normally wore.

"Am I in trouble?" Sam asked.

"Is there something you girls want to tell me?" Mrs. Allen looked from one to the other. "Just because I asked you here doesn't always mean you're in trouble." She paused as the girls both squirmed. Finally, she said, "I need your help."

"With what?" Sam asked.

"The Valentine dance. The committee needs someone's help with the decorating. The chairman felt that since both of you have an artist's eye, you could work together and come up with something spectacular."

"Sam and me?" Emily ran her fingers through her hair. "I don't think we—"

Sam turned to Emily. "Oh, I think we can. After all, we have one major thing in common. We've both been dumped by Eli. Makes us kind of like soul sisters in an über weird sort of way."

"I guess it makes sense, but I'm not planning on going," Emily said. "Who's chairing the committee?"

Mrs. Allen hesitated before answering. "Ava Dawson."

Emily raised her eyebrows and said, "Ava. She wants me to be on the committee? That doesn't make sense."

"Think about it, Emily. It makes a lot of sense," Mrs. Allen responded. "I know there have been some problems since the accident. But I also know for a fact that you haven't lost Ava's friendship. She's just in a bad spot right now. Being on the committee is her way of, well, keeping in touch."

"This is getting more and more interesting," Samantha said. "Come on, Emily, let's do it."

Emily nodded. "Okay, what's next?"

"There's a meeting this afternoon. After school, in the library. Can you girls make it?" Mrs. Allen asked.

"Sure, I wouldn't miss it," said Sam.

"I'm in." Emily stood up and looked at Sam as they exited Mrs. Allen's office. "Cute outfit."

"Thanks. I decided it was time to put away my slutty clothes and change my image. I found that too much partying led me to—you know where."

"So you do remember me from that day in court?" Emily asked. "Why didn't you say anything?"

"It wasn't any of my business." Sam turned and headed down the hallway.

Entering the library after school, Emily heard chatter coming from the far side. She watched as Ava stood to gain control of the meeting. Samantha sat at the end of the table; Emily took an empty seat beside her.

Ava looked at the group and said, "Let's get started. We have a lot of planning ahead of us if this is going to come off. I want to thank Sam and Emily for joining us. They are the decorating committee."

For the next four weeks, Emily's life revolved around driving lessons, preparing for the Valentine dance, and finally understanding algebra. There was no time for moping.

Each day, after school, Father Ron picked her up for a lesson.

"What do you mean the church parking lot?" she said as she threw her backpack onto the seat.

"You think I'm going to let you loose on the streets? No way!" Father Ron put the car in Drive and headed for St. Jude's.

Each day, after her driving lesson, Father Ron would drop her off at Samantha's house.

Samantha's mother always had a snack prepared for the girls. Paper and pencils littered the kitchen table, and designs of all types were taped to the walls as the pair decided which would be best. Red and black dominated their thoughts. Pink was too girly for high school.

Instead of the corny seventies mirrored ball, large tinsel hearts would hang from the ceiling. A black tablecloth would adorn the refreshment table, with assorted balloons on each end. And an iridescent white foil curtain would hang from the entrance.

"I think we should include these purple hanging hearts." Emily pointed to the catalog.

"Are you sure we should add one more color?" Sam asked.

"We have enough money in the budget, and I think it would add another dimension."

"Okay, sounds like a plan."

Each night, Emily filled Da-Shawn and Miki in on her day.

"I even made Father Ron swear today." Emily giggled.

"Not our holy pastor!" Da-Shawn placed his hand over his heart, feigning dismay.

"Oh yeah." Then Emily deepened her voice. "'Jesus, Joseph, and Mary! You almost sideswiped that car, Emily. Watch where you're going.'" Emily started to laugh. "I'm going to see if he knows stronger cuss words tomorrow."

And each night, she wrote in her journal,

> I saw Eli today. He passed by so close to me I could almost smell the musky scent of his cologne. I wanted to say hi but looked the other way and pretended I didn't see him. I'm afraid he hates me.

> Samantha and I are getting to be good friends. She has changed a lot since I first saw her. Wonder what's up with that.

"You're so different than when I first met you," Emily said as they were roaming the party store searching for supplies.

"How do you mean?" Samantha picked up some red cardboard hearts and held them up. "What do you think?"

"Too lame," Emily said. Then she shrugged. "You seemed so stuck-up when we first met."

"I was stuck-up, but it was a way of keeping people away." Sam put the hearts back.

"And then there was that day at the art fair."

"When I saw you with Eli, I was jealous. After all, he was my boyfriend."

"So what happened?" Emily asked.

"My lawyer didn't exactly get me off like I told you he would when we were in court. I was ordered to attend a substance abuse program. I hated it at first, but then I started to listen, and I met some pretty awesome people. I learned a lot about myself and my family, especially my mom."

"What do you mean?" Emily asked.

"I hated her for divorcing my dad. I took all my anger out on her. But I found out my dad had a substance abuse problem, big time. She didn't divorce him. He left us."

Emily nodded. "I know where you're coming from. My mom walked out on me and my dad."

"That sucks," Sam said. "I'm in a twelve-step program. It really helps me keep my head on straight and make good decisions. There is a program for the family. My mom goes. Maybe someday you could go with her."

Emily shook her head. "I know. Father Ron has one at St. Jude's. He keeps trying to get me to go, but I don't think it's for me."

CHAPTER 33

"Nervous?" Da-Shawn asked.

"Well, yeah. Wouldn't you be?" Emily wiped her sweaty hands on her jeans. Her foot wiggled to the boring tune playing from an unknown radio sitting on an unknown desk at the DMV office.

"Anderson." Emily jumped when she heard her name.

She stood up. "Here."

The unsmiling police officer said, "Follow me."

Emily trailed behind her as they proceeded toward Miki's car. She pulled her keys from her purse and pushed the button to unlock the doors. The officer opened the passenger door and slid in. Emily took a deep breath before opening the driver's side and climbing in.

The large woman fastened her seatbelt and held up a clipboard. "Don't be nervous," she said, still unsmiling. "Just follow my instructions."

Emily's hands trembled as she tried to turn the key and start the car.

"Relax. I want you to exit and turn right onto the boulevard."

Emily nodded and proceeded as instructed. She glanced over at the DMV building to see Da-Shawn standing by the window, watching.

When they returned, Da-Shawn was still gazing out the window. Emily parked and got out of the car. Her face set in a frown, she looked at Da-Shawn and shrugged.

He stepped out of the building. "What happened? It was the parallel parking, wasn't it? I told Father Ron you needed more practice."

Emily laughed, pulled a piece of paper she had hidden behind her back, and said, "I did it! I passed."

"That was a dirty trick, Em. You had me there." He gave her a big hug and said, "Let me text Miki. She's got a cake waiting for us. Today's a day for celebrating."

"I have to get my picture taken. I sure hope mine doesn't look as bad as yours."

"Hey now. I think I look a bit like Jamie Foxx," Da-Shawn replied.

"More like Steven Tyler with an Afro." Emily giggled as she opened the door to the DMV.

Two weeks later, Emily pulled into the parking space next to Sam's car.

"I can't believe Miki let you drive her car," Sam said.

"Da-Shawn had a fit. But Miki said it was time to let go and trust." She grinned. "After all, a priest taught me to drive. There should be something in that."

Sam laughed.

Emily shut the door, and the girls walked into the school. They found Ava in the gym with her hands on her hips.

"I never thought you'd get here. Where in the world does all the stuff go?"

Emily set out the plans as Ava started to direct the volunteers.

"I'll hang the hearts from the ceiling. Where is the ladder?" Emily asked.

"Right here."

She turned to see Eli entering the gym carrying a tall ladder. "Why don't you let me do it? I'm taller. And besides, if you fall and break your arm again, I will miss my dance with you." He tilted his head and smiled.

"I wasn't planning on coming to the dance."

"How come?" asked Eli.

"I...I...I don't have a date," Emily said as she handed Eli a heart.

"Neither do I," he said as he climbed up the ladder. "Maybe we could go together."

"You and me? Are you sure?" Butterflies fluttered in Emily's stomach. "What about your parents?"

"Let me take care of them. So, will you go?"

Emily opened her mouth to speak, but all she could do was nod.

The night of the dance, Da-Shawn let out a whistle. "You look beautiful, Em."

"I can't believe we found someone who agreed to sew the dress in such a short time," Miki said.

Emily twirled to show off her own design. She had sketched a dress the day Eli asked her to the dance. It was a short velvet black A-line with lacy sleeves. She wore the necklace he had given her for Christmas with a pair of sterling earrings Miki and Da-Shawn had presented to her earlier that day.

"I wore them the day Da-Shawn and I got married," Miki had said when she handed Emily the small box. "Joy was supposed to wear them at her wedding."

Emily stood staring at them. "Are you sure? They—" she stuttered. "You should keep them for someone else in the family." Emily started to hand them back to Miki.

"You are family, Em," Miki said as she closed her hands around Emily's.

Uninvited tears formed in the corners of Emily's eyes.

To lighten the mood Da-Shawn grabbed the camera. "Look here, girl, we need some pictures. Stand next to Miki."

"I can't believe Eli and I are going to the dance. We haven't talked for, like, forever."

"What?" Miki said. "You were on the phone with him all day. You should have seen her multitask, Da-Shawn. This girl can put on lipstick and text all at the same time."

Da-Shawn kept clicking. "Give me a smile, Em. Eli will be here any minute. We need some pictures for your dad."

Click.

Emily smiled. The doorbell rang.

Eli stood staring. "You look so, so…so amazing, Em."

"Come in here, boy, before you freeze." Da-Shawn motioned to Eli. "We need to get some pictures of the two of you."

Emily rolled her eyes. "We need to humor Da-Shawn." She grabbed Eli's hand and pulled him into the living room.

"Oh, these are for you." Eli handed her a box containing a corsage of pink sweetheart roses. "I think you wear them on your wrist. At least that's what Ava said. She helped me pick them out."

Emily opened the box, took out the flowers, and slipped them on.

"One more picture before you go."

Click, click, click.

"Enough, D-Shawn. You said one more. That was three." Emily walked to the closet and got her coat.

"Can't have enough of you, pretty girl." His face turned somber as he looked at Eli. "Remember to wear your seatbelt, drive slowly, be careful; she is precious cargo."

Eli saluted. "Yes, sir. I've learned my lesson."

"Call us if there is a problem." Miki put her arm around Da-Shawn's waist, looking equally concerned.

The sound of music and teen chatter bounced off the walls of the gym as Eli parted the silver fringed curtain that hung at the entrance.

Before they stepped in, Emily stopped. "Wait," she said. "I need to text Miki and Da-Shawn or they will worry all night." *We r here.* She pushed the send button.

Emily felt Eli's hand on the small of her back as he guided her toward the refreshment table. "Thirsty?"

"Not yet," she said. "Let's look for Ava and Sam first."

"No date for my poor sister." Eli stood on his tiptoes and looked around the crowd.

"Or Sam. I think they both were too busy putting this together. Didn't they do an awesome job?"

Eli nodded. "Come on, let's dance. We'll see them later."

Emily felt the warmth of Eli's embrace as the music slowed and they began to dance. She rested her head on his shoulder.

He whispered something that Emily strained to hear. "You what?" she asked.

"I think I'm falling in love with you," he said louder.

"Love? With me?" She stepped back so she could see his face, but he leaned in and kissed her.

"Busted." Ava stood with a cell phone in her hand. "Oh what a great blackmail pic," she said.

Samantha stood next to Ava with her hands on her hips. She smiled. "Hey, can I cut in?"

"Not a chance," said Emily.

"We're serving punch." Ava pointed to the corner of the gym. "Come over when you two love birds get a chance."

Ava snapped one more picture before she and Sam walked away.

Eli returned Emily's gaze.

"But your parents. They hate me."

He shook his head. "They don't hate you. They are trying to understand what you have been through. They aren't as judgmental as you think. It'll take time."

Emily felt her cheeks flush. Everything was happening so fast. Love seemed foreign to her. She knew Dad loved her, but the addiction smothered it until he found sobriety. If Mom loved her, why did she leave? Mothers were supposed to love their children. And Danny. Oh how she loved her brother, but when he died the grief, the pain, the guilt was more than she could bear. Eli loved her? She looked up at him as he stood there, so close, looking at her…waiting…for her to…what…say I love you, too? *Do I really know how to love?* Emily thought.

Before she could speak, the pace of the music quickened and people swarmed the dance floor, nudging between her and Eli. She spun around wondering what to do. Then, she felt an arm around her waist. "Let's get out of here for a few minutes." Eli pulled her toward the door.

As they walked past Mr. Hunt's door, Eli stepped into the small alcove. Emily followed. "I remember being here once before," she said.

Eli smiled. "This is where we first kissed." He ran one finger gently along the side of her face as he leaned in to kiss her once again.

Emily closed her eyes, inhaling the spicy aroma of his cologne as she felt his lips meet hers. Her heartbeat quickened. This is what she wanted, love and warmth and safety and happiness. When they parted her eyes flew open. "OMG, Eli, I love you, too."

They held each other and kissed once again.

Cheering sounds traveled down the hallway. "What in the world is going on?" Emily thought the entire school must have seen them.

"It's the crowning of the Valentine Sweethearts. Do you want to go back in the gym?" Eli stepped into the hallway.

Emily nodded.

As they entered, they saw Sam sitting on a folding chair decorated with hearts and streamers. She was wearing a crown on her head. In the other chair sat the captain of the basketball team. Emily put her hand to her mouth to stifle a giggle. "Sam isn't even dating. What's that all about?"

Eli laughed. "Looks like she may have found herself a new boyfriend."

"Come on, let's congratulate them," Emily said.

They walked across gym to greet the royal couple. Eli bowed deeply and said, "Congratulations, oh, great queen." He kissed her hand as Emily laughed. Then he turned and fist-bumped his teammate.

Emily bent down and hugged Sam. "You look amazing. Congratulations!"

Samantha waved her hand in a royal gesture. "Thank you, my humble servants. Find a table so I can get away from all this. Being royalty is exhausting. Now I know how Kate Middleton feels."

Eli and Emily hurried over to an empty table near the refreshment table. He pulled a chair out for her. "It's about time you two got here. Where have you been?" They looked up to see Ava arrive with cups of punch.

"Exploring the halls." Eli winked at Emily.

"I'll bet you were exploring more than that. Is that lipstick on your cheek, brother?"

Before he could answer, Sam plunked down in a chair beside Ava. "I am so over all this."

"What happened to the girl who could party all night?" Eli asked.

Sam smiled. "She found a better way of life."

"I totally understand," said Emily.

After the dance Eli drove Emily home. They lingered at the door. "I don't want the evening to end." He bent down and kissed her goodnight.

"Miki and Da-Shawn are probably waiting up for me. I should get in."

"See you tomorrow?" Eli asked.

Emily nodded before kissing him one more time. "Tomorrow."

When she entered the house she found Miki and Da-Shawn asleep on the sofa. Before waking them up, she thought about the last year and how far she'd come. She silently thanked them—for warmth, love, protection.

Home sweet home.

The wisdom to know the difference.

Emily reached behind her and grabbed the seat belt. She clicked it into place and put the key in the ignition. Before starting the car, she looked over at Da-Shawn.

"Would you relax? I had a good teacher. Do you need to see my license again?"

Da-Shawn tightened his seat belt. "I think Father Ron has sprouted a few gray hairs. Whatever possessed him to teach you to drive?"

Emily looked in the rearview mirror. "Come on, Father, tell him what a good driver I am."

Father Ron laughed.

Miki said, "Enough with all the teasing. This is a big day for Em. Are you ready for this?" She reached out to give Emily a reassuring pat on the shoulder.

Emily nodded and started the car.

The memory of the trip to the courthouse in September lingered in her mind. She shook off thoughts of Frank and his evil grin, the dragon tattoo, and that fear-filled night. Frank was shipped off to prison and not a threat.

Emily pulled into a vacant parking space near the jail. She put the car in Park, turned off the ignition, and then took a deep breath.

No one spoke as they neared the entrance.

Emily was the first one to notice the door opening. She stopped and watched Dad step out. He was dressed in the khaki slacks and the navy, long-sleeved polo shirt she and Miki had purchased at Macy's. She watched him zip up the wool jacket Da-Shawn had loaned him. Even from a distance, she could make out his shiny blond hair parted on the side and combed neatly back. He was sporting a mustache.

Emily started to run. "Dad!"

He sprinted down the concrete steps and caught her up in his arms. He hugged her so tightly Emily thought she would lose her breath. Then he cried.

She tried but couldn't stop her own tears.

He let her go and held her at arm's length. "Wow, Em, you look amazing."

"So do you, Dad." She wiped away the tears.

She watched him pull out a pocket of bills. "My gettin' out of jail money. I think it's just enough for a couple pieces of apple pie. After all, this is a day for celebrating."

"Put your money away, Dad. We're going to have a big 'coming out' party. Miki's got tons of food, and I baked the apple pies. You can meet my best friends Ava and Samantha. And, my boyfriend, Eli."

"If only your mom could be here," Dad said.

Emily nodded.

They turned, hand-in-hand, and walked toward the others.

As they drove away from the jail, Emily spotted a lone car, situated at the other end of the parking lot. There was something familiar about the shadowy figure of the solitary woman sitting in the driver's seat, smoking a cigarette. Emily started to say something to Dad, but he was busy talking to Father Ron.

From the distance, she watched the woman run her fingers through her hair as she turned the ignition to the car, back out, and follow them down the boulevard.